The Canary's Song

Gerald Sloan

Published by Gerald Sloan, 2014.

THE CANARY'S SONG

First edition. August 15, 2014.

ISBN: 979-8201098193

Written by Gerald Sloan.

The Canary's Song

by

Gerald Sloan

Copyright 2014 Gerald Sloan

Prologue

Northern Oaks Nursing and Therapy Center lies tucked in a hillside on the outskirts of Beechwood, Mississippi, just a few miles east of Vicksburg. It is a popular choice for those needing extended or permanent nursing care and are willing to pay for it. One of the newer nursing homes built in the last few years, it is clean and well maintained; traits not always found in long term care facilities. The staff is widely known to be friendly and dedicated to the care of their residents, more so than one would find in a nursing home located in larger cities and towns. Not that the urban homes can't be this way, but in small towns across America, staff in nursing homes find more recognizable faces and family in their buildings therefore they tend to acquire a better sense of fellowship in caring for them.

The entrance into Northern Oaks has a double glass door that opens into a vestibule. One must press a button to unlock the next set of double glass doors before being allowed access to the building. These doors remain locked at all time, not to keep would be criminals out, rather to keep residents that suffer from dementia or other diseases of the brain, in. Once inside, a visitor enters a large common area replete with polished furniture, fine carpeting, and a fireplace on the outside wall. The facility's administrative offices lie to the left and there is a receptionist sitting at a large walnut desk located in front of them to welcome guests and help them find their way in the facility. An ornate chapel lies halfway down the passage that lies to the right.

Northern Oaks is laid out in what is referred to as a "hub and spoke" pattern. Three long corridors radiate from the front common area and arrive at hexagonal shaped nursing station areas where five more resident halls, or wings, branch out. All the hallways, with exception of the two front access halls which provide access to the chapel, dining and activities rooms, have resident rooms. A nurse's station acts as the hub of responsibility for the residents that reside in the halls adjacent to their station. The two hubs to the right and left connect to the third that lies to the back of the facility, thus creating a diamond shape as seen from above. It can serve nearly 300 residents and its census rarely falls below full capacity.

Far from Northern Oaks' status in quality of care, cleanliness, and distance is a Medicaid funded alternative. Coventry Nursing Center is located in the heart of Vicksburg and is subsidized by Mississippi Medicaid and other meager funding sources that are available. The staff in this facility doesn't lack in their willingness to serve and help their residents, but they operate on a thread bare budget and are over-worked. Whereas an Registered Nurse, (RN), at Northern Oaks may care for a dozen residents on a daily case load, a Coventry RN may have twice that many. The Licenced Practical Nurse, or LPN's, and aides are short staffed as well and have the low morale that accompanies being poorly paid combined with too much responsibility. Theirs is an endless morass of inability to completely satisfy residents' needs and desires.

Because Coventry is small, (serving only 105 residents), in comparison to other nursing homes, it is laid out in a square format with a small courtyard in the middle. Each hallway connects to a corner where a small nurse's station stands. Barely three caregivers can fit behind the station at the same time so nurses and aides jostle over each other to retrieve patient charts from the shelves that line the exterior wall. The hallways are filled with residents removed from their bedrooms to give them social time and allow nurses and aides easy visibility to inspect their well-being. The hallways are painted a drab ivory that due to the nursing home's age appear to have been repainted dozens of times thus lending a shiny thickness to the paint. The floors of linoleum squares have lost their luster but still remain polished enough to look acceptable. The facility's design does nothing to separate odors from one corridor to another; therefore, a walk through the facility never gives a visitor a respite from the fetor of incontinence and disease. While Coventry must meet State standards and regulations to remain viable, it barely does so and the result is a health care facility with a mortality and bed sore rate higher than the State average.

Like any housing in America, Nursing Home environments vary drastically depending on the financial well-being of those who inhabit them. Poorer facilities make do with State appropriated funding and provide adequate care to those who cannot afford higher levels of care. Higher end facilities offer services and accommodations worthy of five star hotels. The great majority, however, lie somewhere in between these two extremes. One thing all these facilities have in common is an overwhelming commitment to the health and welfare of those who must reside in them.

Chapter 1

"From caring comes courage." —Lao Tzu

Matitha Williams stared out the bus window and into the darkness, looking past the stranger sitting directly across the aisle. She was tired and the recent Day Light Savings Time adjustment didn't help. The 5:45am bus and its bleary-eyed occupants were just beginning to see daylight as the darkness of winter slowly eroded into spring but the small incremental gains were thrust back by the jolt of setting the clock ahead one hour. Losing an hour of sleep is difficult on the body and even more so for Matitha. She tried going to bed earlier the last few nights to no avail. She merely spent the hour lying awake tossing in bed, doing crossword puzzles until she fell asleep at her usual time, albeit one hour later by the clock. That, coupled by the darkness of the morning hour, made leaving her bed that much more difficult.

Matitha shared her home with her older sister, Lucinda, and her son, Jamal. She was grateful that her older sister lived with her and her boy, Byron. Lucinda worked a regular nine-to-five schedule and saw to it that both boys arrived safely at the elementary school's early arrival care center to start the school day. Matitha could pick the boys up after her shift ended thus making sure that neither boy was ever home unattended. The sisters were committed to giving their boys every advantage they had missed growing up in the inner city of Vicksburg. Although they had escaped to decent paying jobs and a home in the suburbs, they were acutely aware of the darker sides of life that could suck in a young African-American boy and send his life careening down a path of drugs and violence. It required relentless vigilance and patience that on a normal day simply left Matitha tired at bedtime. However, Day Light Savings Time was the worst day of the year as it compounded the weariness.

Today's fatigue is coupled with dread and the adrenaline rush that accompanies it. Her yawns of exhaustion punctuate her nervous fidgeting. Her favorite patient, Mary Stuart, had elected months ago to participate in physician-assisted suicide today. Matitha understood the reasoning behind Mary's decision, but she didn't like it. She was adamantly against self-euthanasia for spiritual reasons, as well as, the effect it had on caregivers like herself. Matitha had dedicated her life to helping the victims of aging and late-life disease. Having someone consciously rip himself or herself from her care hurt her pride.

Of course, letting go of patients was easier with some than others. Even though she had always been dedicated to the proposition of love thy neighbor, some people were so difficult to deal with that, despite herself, she was relieved when they were gone. However, Mary didn't fall into that category. Matitha recalled with rare clarity the day that brought Mary into her life. Mary transferred from an Assisted-Living Home to Northern Oaks and was assigned to Matitha's hall. She recalled how timid and unsure Mary was in the beginning. The range of motion in her limbs was better then and she could manage to feed and clean herself to some degree but her abilities were fading fast and she needed therapy and more assistance with daily activities than she could rely on in an assisted-living environment. Mary tried so hard not to be a burden on the staff, always apologizing when she called them and insisting that they care for others first whose needs were greater than hers. Her unselfishness was refreshing to Matitha and reminded her of her own mother who had died nearly ten years to the day of a heart attack. As her affection grew for Mary and she saw more traits in her that reminded Matitha of her mother, she took to calling Mary, "Mama," out of respect and love for her.

Matitha knew that Mary's situation was complicated. Not only was she in severe pain most of the time, but her personal savings had been exhausted and she was being forced to move from Northern Oaks to Coventry Nursing Center, a State funded facility located in the center of Vicksburg. Matitha knew from stories and visits there that Mary wouldn't fare well in that home. Mary had always enjoyed a middle class, white man's world with very little exposure to the harsher side of being poor. Going to a facility that was 90% minority, marginally clean, and lacking in the personal care Mary was used to, would depress Mary and add another element of misery to her remaining days. Matitha had promised Mary that she would visit her regularly but both knew that Matitha's time was stretched as it was and although she would never back off her promise to visit, the visits would be, by necessity, short and infrequent—not quite enough to ask Mary to endure the hardships she would face at Coventry.

Regardless, Matitha didn't want Mary to follow through with her plans. Mary brought so much joy to the staff at Northern Oaks that she was certain she would do the same for Coventry. Knowing that life was difficult for Mary, Matitha thought about how strenuous her own childhood was and how it would have been easier to give in to the temptations of drugs and alcohol like a great majority of her friends. Other than her mother, nobody expected an inner-city girl to rise out of the dregs of humanity and make something of her life. Matitha believed in her mother and God's plan and knew she must endure the hardships to fulfill her purpose. The same should be true for Mary. If she's still capable of bringing joy to others lives, which she does daily, then she should live the entire lifespan God intended for her. Watching the street lights and neon signs flick past her as the bus travelled down the street, Matitha was reminded how life is nothing more than a bus ride traveling a timeline with many stops and destinations, scenes of joy and sorrow, comfort, and at times, pain. However, one doesn't jump off while the bus is still moving.

Resolving that she still had time to change Mary's mind, Matitha took the last few minutes of the ride to think of ways and arguments that might be effective with Mary. Bouncing between overreaching thoughts of hope, and pangs of loss if Mary does follow through, Matitha brushed her hand across her cheek to catch the tear that had began to run down it. She caught it before it dropped, perhaps a good omen that she can do the same for Mary.

****

The room is still dark. Only the steady rise and fall of deep exhalations from a sleeping occupant break the silence. Two beds separated by a thin curtain hanging from ceiling rails give the room a false sense of privacy. Modest personal mementos such as family photos, ceramic treasures, and clocks adorn the small nightstands standing next to each bed. The walls are bare except for the window at the far end of the room. Strips of light shimmer between the slats of the blinds, lowered to darken the room. Like a luminescent ladder ascending the wall, the light gives notice of the day beginning outside. In this facility, the passing of day into night and night into day can go unnoticed by some of its occupants even as daylight radiates the rooms and passages. It is not the light that cannot be seen, however, it is the lost understanding of what it means that tortures the souls of many in this place.

Mary Stuart is not one of these. She knows very well what the implication of the light means, as hers is not a disability of the mind. Rather, it is her body that has betrayed her. Mary was admitted here because arthritis and other ailments had so ravished her body that she could no longer do more than weakly raise her arms. She had lost the ability to walk nearly a decade ago. A wheelchair became her constant companion as she navigated daily life in her home. However, over time, her shoulders and hands slowly acquiesced to the pain and stiffness leaving her sitting with limited ability to care for herself. Having no family, Mary remained in her assisted-living apartment as long as she could, relying on the staff to get her to her meals and help change her adult diapers on occasions. But as her condition worsened, she was deemed incapable of living with minimal assistance and was accepted here, the Northern Oaks Nursing and Therapy Center.

Mary now lay quietly in her bed staring at the light in the window, waiting for her LPN to come in and get her ready for the day. She shares her room with another resident, Laura something..., as she couldn't recall having ever heard Laura's last name spoken. "I wonder if she knows my name?" thought Mary. Laura was one of those residents who either by disease or drug, didn't interact much with anyone. She mumbled from time to time about a son she expected to visit, but he never came. Of course, no one came for Mary either but at least she knew better than to believe that someone would. The highlight of her day was when Matitha, her care nurse, came to ready her for the day.

Matitha is a Licensed Practical Nurse, or LPN. Her short and stocky physique accentuates the ever present smile on her face and song on her lips. She unfailingly glides into the room singing spirituals under her breath and crosses the room to hug Mary before preparing her for breakfast. Why she did this only for Mary was anyone's guess, but to Mary, it meant the world. Mary loves that Matitha refers to her as "Mama" and that she treats her as though she really is her mother. Her words and caring gestures are a constant delight to Mary and the only thing she would deeply miss about this place.

She heard Matitha enter the room as she would recognize the sound of her gait in a hail storm. But Matitha wasn't singing today, nor did she come to the bed and hug Mary as she usually did. Instead, she stopped short of the end of the bed and suddenly turned away from Mary.

"Matitha, are you alright?" croaked Mary in a voice which hinted these were the first words she'd spoken today.

"Mama, I don't want you to see me like this." came the sloppy reply restraining to hold back tears. "I told myself I wasn't gonna be nothin' but happy for you today and I ruint' it already."

"Honey, you are so sweet to me." stammered Mary. "I'm so sorry I'm hurting you. Come hold my hand, please."

Matitha slowly turned towards Mary and began walking to the side of her bed, fully blocking the light from the window blinds. Silhouetted against the window, the light that was sharp and defined between the slats now illuminated Matitha's girth, forming a full halo. The effect and the implications weren't lost on Mary as she knew Matitha to be the only angel left in her life. Matitha took Mary's hand and began rubbing it between her young, strong hands.

"Don't be sad, angel. We knew this day was coming." Mary stated strongly and then paused for a brief moment before continuing. "Of course, with the exception of you, I have no reason to be here anymore."

"But ain't that enough, Mama? I mean, if you really feels the way you says ya do, then you shouldn't go through with this! I think you're making a very bad decision and it hurts me."

"Matitha, we've already been over this. I can't afford to live here anymore. I've exhausted my savings and I'm on the State's dollar now. This place is for those who can afford it and I'm no longer one of those. I abhor the thought of leaving this facility for that one downtown. I won't do it, Matitha"

"I know, Mama, but I'd come visit you. You know I would." Matitha started to cry and her whole body convulsed in the rhythmic shakes that accompanied heavy sobbing.

"I gotta get out of here for a few minutes," she sputtered, "I'll be back when I's better composed."

And with that, she gently laid Mary's hand back on the bed and quickly stumbled out of the room. Mary, frustrated and upset by the encounter, closed her eyes and began thinking of better days.

Chapter 2

"Memories are the key not to the past, but to the future." —Corrie Ten Boom

"Depart now and as you go remember. By the Goodness of God you were born into this world. By the Grace of God you have been kept all the day long, even unto this very hour. And by the Love of God, fully revealed on the face of Jesus, you are being Redeemed!"

"Mom, why does Pastor Johnson end the sermons with that same benediction every time?" asked a young Mary as she and her parents left the First Baptist Church one Spring Sunday.

"Because he doesn't know any others!" quipped her father, Sammy, in his casual wry way.

Samuel Smith, or Sammy, as he was known throughout the community of Buckner, Missouri, was a hard working mechanic at a locally owned gas station. Sammy served in the Army Air Force during World War II working on B-17 bombers at a base in Southern England. Although he never saw direct action in the war, he witnessed the carnage brought back by returning bombers and their sometimes mutilated crews. It didn't take him very long to appreciate how fortunate he was to help fight the war without great physical risk to him. He would often work well beyond his shift to ensure that the planes he maintained were at their very best for the next mission. If he couldn't take it to the Nazis himself, he wanted to know that he had done everything he could to protect those that did. After returning to Buckner from the war, several years went by before he met and married Mary's mother, Christina. It didn't take long for the happy couple to conceive Mary and shortly after they were married, they were a small family. Unfortunately, due to complications during childbirth, Christina was unable to have any more children.

"Sammy, you really shouldn't...one of these days you are going to be struck by lightening and I swear you'll have it coming!" laughed

Christina. "Vengeance is mine sayeth the Lord!" she said blurting out her best imitation of Pastor Johnson. And with this, all three laughed as they walked down the road leading south out of the main square.

After the laughter subsided, Mary brought up the point again. "No, seriously, I like what he says. It makes me feel good. I just don't know why he always ends that way. Isn't he afraid people will get tired of hearing it?"

Done laughing now, her mother paused for a few moments to consider her response. "That's a very good question, Mary. I suppose he's not afraid of that because it is such a nice thing to hear. If we get nothing more from the sermon, at least we have that nice thought to carry us through the week. It makes me feel good too, to know that God has blessed us and watches over us."

In her early teenage years now, Mary was past fidgeting and daydreaming during Pastor Johnson's sermons. She was paying closer attention to his messages with more post-sermon thought. It seemed ironic to her that on many Sundays he would raise the rafters with a fire and brimstone sermon that left every unrepentant soul shaking for fear of an eternal life spent in a blazing inferno. Yet after completing the sermon and obligatory passing of the offering plate, (which seemed a bit heavier on these Sundays), he would end with such a calm and beautiful parting. The juxtaposition between each one left Mary wondering which God watched over her, the vengeful and punitive God ready to punish her at every misstep, or the caring Father who sent his Son into the world to pay for the sins of humanity. It seemed the latter had a better understanding of the human condition and sent a message of hope, not fear, to guide humanity.

"Dad, when you were in the war, did you think about God's blessings? It must have been hard with all the killing going on." Mary inquired of her father.

Sammy didn't answer at first. He stared straight ahead as he walked and was overtaken by a slight shudder that was too controlled to be noticed by his family. His mind instantly went back to a memory of pulling a ball gunner from the bottom of a just-landed bomber. An explosion of anti-aircraft fire had blown away the bottom of the plane just aft of the gunner's position. In doing so, a large piece of metal had nearly split the ball turret in half, leaving the gunner in essence cut in two. However, because of the compactness of the gunner's position, the cold temperatures at altitude, and the wedge of metal acting as pressure on the gruesome wound, the gunner didn't bleed to death but survived the flight back to the base. When Sammy and the other crewmembers arrived to extricate him, they knew he wouldn't survive the maneuver to extract him. They asked him if they could do anything for him before pulling him out and his reply stuck with Sammy to this very day. He whispered, "I'll be fine. I think God's awaitin' on me. Tell my parents I love them." Shortly thereafter, the gunner lost consciousness for the last time.

"Did you hear me, Dad?" asked Mary mistaking her father's concentration on the question and the memory it wrought for neglect.

"Yes, Mary, I did. You asked a very thoughtful question that requires a thoughtful answer. Give me a second to answer it please."

Sammy walked on a few more paces before replying.

"Yes, I did think about God and His blessings a lot while in Europe. I was particularly thankful everyday to have lived another day. But sometimes I wondered why mankind seemed so determined to destroy itself when God showered us with the blessing of life. All those people, good and bad, died during a war that was brought on by one, evil person. It just didn't make sense to me at times and certainly didn't fit well with the message of peace that Jesus sent us. Life is such a precious commodity to waste. God gave it to us and who are we to take it from someone else? I think that is the blessing God gave me to think about and share after the war."

Mary was intrigued by this revelation from her father. He rarely spoke of the war and he never shared any details of what he saw or did over there. She was always surprised when he opened up like this to share his thoughts on the matter. She quietly contemplated what he had said. She wasn't exactly sure what she had wanted as an answer from her dad, but this seemed more cryptic than she expected. After further thought, she realized that it did fit the conversation of the benediction. God's truest blessing is the first blessing of life itself. Her father was right; no one had the right to erase that blessing.

****

"Did you hear me, Mama?" asked Matitha in a very loud voice. "I said, are you ready to get outta bed?"

Mary was jolted back to the present and it took her a moment to regain her bearings.

"I'm sorry, Matitha. What did you say?"

"I said, are you ready to get outta bed?"

Mary winced at the notion of even moving, let alone the arduous task of letting Matitha clean her and Hoyer Lift her out of the bed. She had given up all sense of self-respect when she became reliant upon adult diapers but what little dignity remained quickly dissolved when she could no longer put them on or take them off. Having someone clean her in this regard was as embarrassing as one could imagine. She acquiesced to it several times a day, although not enough to be completely clean and comfortable as the aides were very busy and would only get around to this task as a last resort. Appropriately enough, they hated it as much as Mary.

Matitha began the process as she usually did. She always bent over the bed and hugged Mary before she started. This seemed to help. Then she gently pulled back the covers and began stretching Mary's legs out. Mary didn't know why, but her legs tended to pull up into a fetal position during the night and were very stiff and difficult to straighten in the morning. The pain shot through Mary's body as Matitha pulled her legs. It was as though the muscles in her legs were being torn in two. She let out a small moan that let Matitha know she needed to go slower. Once she had Mary's legs straightened, Matitha would remove her diaper and clean up the urine and fecal material that accumulated during the night. The odor was awful for both Matitha and her but each soldiered on and pretended not to notice.

Matitha stood up, snapped the latex gloves from her hands, and went into the hall to get the Hoyer Lift. The Hoyer Lift reminded Mary of the engine block lifts her father had used in his work shop. Instead of lifting motors, however, this contraption lifted people. Matitha fastidiously fastened the sling around Mary, making sure she left no open snaps or holes that might slip and cause her to plummet to the floor. She then started pumping the handle that hydraulically lifted Mary from the bed. Once Mary was clear of the bedding, Matitha slowly swung the Hoyer lift around, pivoting Mary over her wheelchair. Even this slow swaying motion sent waves of pain through Mary's body. As she aligned with the center of the chair, Matitha turned a knob that released the hydraulic pressure and the machine slowly dropped Mary into it.

The wheelchair that Mary used was a very special kind. It allowed the staff to tilt her at various degrees to help mitigate some of her pain and prevent pressure ulcers from forming on her bottom. This it did very well as Mary had luckily avoided sores. The Therapy Department in the nursing home attributed much of this to the chair but Mary believed equal credit be shared with the staff that came and tilted the chair regularly. She could only tolerate any one position for about an hour before she needed tilted to a new angle. Her favorite position in the chair was one where it was fully tilted back. She felt like an astronaut ready for take-off when in this position. It was also the only position that she could bear for more than an hour. The downside, however, was that she couldn't do much more than stare at the ceiling due to the extreme angle of tilt. Mary often wondered why life never seemed to offer compromise. At least hers, anyway.

"Mama, let's get you down to the dining room before they stop servin'. I took too long with you today and you shouldn't miss breakfast cuz of me."

"Okay, Matitha. If you say so. It really doesn't matter to me. I don't have much appetite." Mary said forlornly.

Matitha looked at her with the sarcastic frown she used on such occasions and replied, "Is it cuz the pain? I have yo' meds right here ifin' you want 'em. I think it's foolish of you to bear all the pain just cuz it's your last day. You should at least take some to take the edge off."

Mary quickly responded with a rare show of agitation, "I'm NOT going to spend my final moments drugged up, Matita! I want to feel the pain to remind me why I'm doing what I'm doing today."

Matitha sadly shook her head and let the subject drop. She began pushing Mary out of her room and into the hallway. It was already busy with the hustle and bustle of a new day. RN's were sitting at the nurse's station looking over the patient charts and reading new physician orders that may have come across their desk since their last shift. Aides were walking quickly to and fro assisting residents with their various morning needs and activities. In fact, an aide should have been pushing Mary to the Dining Hall, but Matitha would have none of that on her last day with Mary.

"Mama, are you sure you're doing the right thing? I know I'm not s'posed to talk about it anymore but I can't help it. I don't think it's what we should do. God makes His plans for us and it ain't our place to change 'em."

Mary didn't answer Matitha.

Chapter 3

"Hope is the thing with feathers that perches in the soul - and sings the tunes without the words - and never stops at all." —Emily Dickenson

Tabitha Adams woke with her usual morning headache. She'd been experiencing them for nearly four months. She was not the kind of person who believed that every ache and pain was a sign of a far worse ailment but she couldn't overlook the fact that these headaches were a bit too regular to explain. She visited a doctor a week earlier and after a full exam and questioning, he dismissed the morning headaches as the result of stress and possibly depression. He prescribed Paxil, gave her some relaxation exercises and asked that she follow up with him in two to four weeks. After six days of taking the medication and ignoring the relaxation exercises, she hadn't improved any. "Ugh," she thought to herself. "is this rock bottom or what?"

Tabitha lived in a small flat on the west side of Vicksburg, not far from the two major highways that bisected it. She didn't have much furniture; the futon she slept on, a small end table, and a dining table with four chairs were the culmination of her adult acquisitions. She had all that she needed though, and most importantly, all that she could afford. She didn't have a television, nor was she willing to pay for it, so she watched old TV shows on her computer tablet to pass the endless hours of nothingness that had overtaken her life.

Mack, her boyfriend since she had left Ole Miss as a sophomore, had left her seven months ago and she was still rebounding. She couldn't shake the memories of meeting him on campus at a Homecoming event and instantly falling for him. He was a senior then, graduating from the Business School that spring and the thoughts of running off with him to start a life together began to drip into her thoughts and desires. While their relationship didn't explode in the first few months they were together, it quickly gained momentum after winter break. The few weeks they were apart seemed to have driven them both crazy; to the point that when they returned to school, they were both primed for a very deep and meaningful relationship.

As Mack's graduation approached, so did conversations about what was going to happen to them afterward. Mack had been interviewing with a company in New Orleans that seemed very interested in hiring him. However, he wasn't keen on the idea of being that far away from Tabitha, nor was she. After a few "what if" discussions, they agreed that Mack should take the job in New Orleans if an offer was made and she would relocate there to finish her degree. The job offer came, and by mid-July, they were both living in a nice apartment in the stylish Garden District of New Orleans.

The first two years were nearly magical in every sense. They quickly made friends and enjoyed the endless partying that the city is well-known for. They would take long walks along the historic streets and canals, breathing in all that the sights and sounds had to offer. They embraced the Saints football tradition in the city and managed to find tickets to nearly every game. Most importantly, they relished the New Orleans music scene and spent many evenings at different clubs listening to the "real" jazz New Orleans is famous for while avoiding the over-hyped French Quarter.

Trouble, however, began brewing after Mack was promoted to a national sales position. He began to make more money and seemed to be uncomfortable sharing it with Tabitha. He started making biting remarks about her lowly financial contributions to the relationship and asking her when she was going to finish college. They had been having such a good time up to this point that she had nearly given up on getting her degree. Her job at a bookstore and their nights on the town sufficiently satisfied her. His sudden interest and desire to see her finish school confused and worried her.

She began to press Mack about marriage and he seemed to get better for a while. They both enjoyed talking about building a family together in the suburbs and joining PTA's. They imagined old row houses separated by white picket fences in neighborhoods where everyone knew each other. They envisioned going to block parties and watching their kids play with the other neighborhood kids. But after several months of this kind of dreaming, Mack began to appear distant again and recommenced his nasty comments. Tabitha attributed his attitude to the stress of nearly constant travel and thought a long vacation in the Bahamas would help them both. After a week in tropical paradise, they came home and Mack left her.

He had neither the heart, nor the courage to tell her in person. He left town on a business trip, called her on her cell phone when she couldn't answer it at work, and left a rambling excuse about how she deserved better and that he wasn't the guy for her. He said that he would be gone for a few weeks and asked that she leave the apartment, taking anything she wanted before he returned.

Naturally, Tabitha was heartbroken and confused. She loved Mack and didn't want it to end with him. She thought that perhaps this was just a stage he was going through and that he would come back home and reconsider. So instead of taking any of the belongings they had acquired together, she left and moved in with another couple they had been friends with for the past few years. Night after night she waited for Mack to call. She spent many late evenings with her friends, whom Mack had apparently abandoned too, trying to ascertain what on earth had happened. Speculations abounded but didn't really help much with the reality of the situation. After nearly six months of waiting, Tabitha gave up and decided to move back to her hometown in Vicksburg. On her last night in New Orleans, she wandered off into the French Quarter to visit one of the seedy tattoo dives that populated every street in the district. After much deliberation, she chose to mark herself with a tattoo that would remind her of the beast a man could be.

****

Despite her headache, Tabitha was looking forward to her new job today at Northern Oaks Nursing and Rehab. Since returning to Vicksburg, she had been working as a waitress at a Denny's restaurant to make ends meet until she could find something else to do. She just wasn't certain what that something else was. Tired of working night and weekend shifts, she had begun perusing Craigslist looking for a different job that would have more regular hours. She had come across the Northern Oaks listing looking for aides to work in the Nursing Home's Kitchen and Dining Room and thought that might be a great diversion for her. Although the pay wasn't much better than minimum wage, as she explained to her mom, "what better way to feel better about yourself than hanging out with people way less fortunate than you?"

With the attitude that she was going to help people in need and make a difference in life, Tabitha soared through the nursing home's orientation and training. Her supervisor, a young woman who'd graduated from Ole Miss with a degree in Dietetics and Nutrition, ten years earlier, instantly bonded with Tabitha and told her about the special people she would be assisting. She made the job sound very interesting and Tabitha was eager to get started.

Looking in the mirror after the morning shower's steam had finally disappeared, Tabitha noticed for the first time how pallid and thin her face had become. She had lost slightly more than twenty pounds in the past six months but like mold growing on bread, she didn't see it until it was right in front of her. Her eyes appeared sunken with gray lines emanating from the corners and arching down her cheeks. Her mouse brown hair was hanging unevenly with ragged split ends from months of neglect. In short, her image manifested the worn out soul she had become.

She smiled in the mirror as she considered how badly she looked and almost instantly, the shameful shell she'd become evaporated, replaced by a bright-eyed, albeit thin, seraph.

"Wow," she said out loud to no one, "what a difference! I'll just have to smile all day..."

She applied what meager amounts of makeup she still had, focusing almost extensively on the lines under her eyes. She pulled her hair into a pony tail, donned her uniform, which was nothing more than the scrubs all the nurses and aides wore in the nursing home, and went into the kitchenette area in a vain attempt to eat some breakfast. She opened a cabinet door, stared into the emptiness of the cabinet and grabbed the lone jar of peanut butter that stood there. Snatching a large spoon from a drawer, she drove it deep into the jar and brought forth a mound of peanut butter that she quickly shoved into her mouth. She slid over to the refrigerator and stared at a picture of her and Mack under a magnet as she slurped and gulped the mass of peanut butter in her mouth. After she had swallowed several times to clear her throat, she reached for a glass and filled it with water. Drinking half of it, she poured the rest in the sink, grabbed her car keys and left.

Since she lived so close to the highway that connected her apartment and Northern Oaks, the drive was a quick one against the morning traffic. Like girls her age are wont to do, she drove with the radio playing loudly, bobbing her head every once in a while to a song she really liked. She scanned the scenery she had passed dozens of time in her life and noted that nothing had really changed. It appeared the mundane houses and businesses that lined the highway were the same ones she remembered as a little girl. However, everything seemed different at this stage of her life. After living a few years at college followed by the whirlwind that was New Orleans, she felt much older and introspective, leaving the little girl of wonderment and possibilities far behind. The small houses now looked unkempt and depressing, as if their occupants had given up on their lives and the houses were bold statements to that fact. The businesses had meaning to her now. A muffler or tire shop seemed important to remember for times in need, while gas stations were noted for their convenience for future use.

After exiting the highway, she drove a few blocks before coming to the entrance to Northern Oaks. Although the hour was early, there were already too many cars in the parking lot. Tabitha was unaware that shift changes caused near havoc in the parking area. While there were plenty of spaces for employees to park, the spaces were taxed when new shifts arrived to take the parking spaces of employees who hadn't left yet. She made a few passes through each row, hoping to find an empty spot but was left frustrated when she found none. Growing impatient and worried that she would be late on her first day, she gave up on the employee lot and drove to the front of the building where the visitor's parking area resided. She had been specifically told in orientation not to park in the visitor's lot, but rationalized it by the fact that nobody should recognize her car this first day and that she would move it on her first break. Clearly, she thought, she'd better arrive earlier tomorrow.

After she settled into a spot furthest from the front door, she turned off her ignition and sat with both hands on the steering wheel. Slightly shaken by the unexpected delay in parking, Tabitha wanted to clear her head before entering the building. She turned off her radio and breathed deeply in slow, steady draws. Although this was one of the relaxation techniques she had been taught to calm herself, she did it instinctively today without any thought as to why. She spent a few seconds staring at the building and then resigned herself to the fact that it was time to enter it. While excited about the job, she was nervous about what lay ahead of her. "Who are these people," she thought, "and where do I fit into their lives?"

Chapter 4

"Find a place inside where there's joy, and the joy will burn out the pain."
—Joseph Campbell

As a seventeen year old, Mary had matured into a very pretty high school senior. Although it was the early '70's, the hippy movement and its sloppy, bedraggled dress style hadn't made its way to Buckner. She and her friends still wore dresses to school from time to time and maintained a decorum that was a little out of step with the rapidly changing times. That was perfectly fine by Mary. She had no desire to change the world and was perfectly content to live out her life in the sanctity of their small and wonderful community. Images of the Vietnam War were broadcast on the three television stations their antenna could pick up but the war seemed surreal and unaffecting to Mary, even though she stylishly wore a POW bracelet on her wrist. It wasn't a popular war with most people and Mary's family was no exception. Other news of national interest seemed dull or painful to hear, so Mary and her family lived happily oblivious to most things occurring outside a thirty mile radius of their town.

Mary and her two best friends were riding in her father's car, heading into Independence to dress shop for the school's upcoming dance. They were very excited because this was the first dance of their final year in High School. Additionally, it was a Sadie Hawkins dance which required them to ask a boy to go with them. All three knew who they were going to ask and were giggling and laughing at each other's practice invitations.

"I think it's silly we have to ask boys to these dances!" complained Debbie from the front passenger seat of the car.

Debbie Shanihan never hurt for boys' attention. A petite, blue eyed blond, with a charming dimple on her left cheek, Debbie could date any boy she desired. In fact, she had dated almost every boy in their graduating class at some point since Junior High School. Although she had dated a lot, nobody considered her "easy" as she usually dated a boy once and then moved on. She was the girl that no boy expected to ever get as a girlfriend so they stopped thinking of her in this way. Instead, she was the girl that everyone liked to take to dances when they couldn't find a date that was interested in them. She would be fun and always accepting of a kiss goodnight and that was it. For most boys at this age, that was enough.

"I mean, why do we go through this every year?" she continued. "It's such a pain trying to pick someone to go with!"

"Oh, really Debbie? We're going to pretend to be sad because you have too many boys to choose from?" Mary countered and laughed out loud. "Why don't you ask Borin' Orin Thatcher? I'm sure his daddy would let him come out of the cow pastures to escort you! He can wear that nice suede coat that looks like the cows he raises!"

This set all three girls laughing so hard that Mary nearly swerved off the road. Cindy Lewis was sitting between the two girls in the front seat and jutted her hand into her crotch.

"Stop it! I'm gonna pee my pants!" she said and the girls laughed even harder.

Cindy had been Mary's best friend since Kindergarten. They lived a few blocks away from each other and had spent almost every free moment together since then. She too, was a pretty girl with long dark auburn hair but a bit stockier in build than Mary and Debbie.

After the laughter subsided some, Cindy looked straight out in front of the car and took on a serious tone.

"Do you think Don Shuler will go with me?" she muttered.

"He'd better," stated Debbie matter-of-factly, "or I'll have my brother nail him in wrestling!"

"Debbie, you wouldn't! I don't want a boy going with me cuz he got the tar whipped outta him. Promise me you won't say anything!"

"I wouldn't, you know that. Besides, I heard from Kathy, who heard from her boyfriend, Steve, that Don has a thing for you. You shouldn't worry whether he goes with you but how *far* he tries to go with you!"

And again, the girls were laughing hysterically as they drove down Interstate 70. Mary smiled inwardly at all the good times she had with these two friends. They had talked about every "first" they had ever had and made fun of each other as soon as they did. There was no sanctity in their friendship when they were together. Everything was fair game to be poked fun at and most evenings ended in pure exhaustion from the laughing. More than once, their parents had checked their rooms for alcohol or marijuana because they couldn't understand what the girls found so funny. But theirs was that rare bond where the different personalities fit perfectly. They each shared their heartbreaks and tragedies, too, but only in one-on-one sessions as the group was made for good times.

"It must be nice for Mary, having Ted lined up already. Do you even have to ask him, or is it just assumed at this point in your relationship?" asked a giggling Debbie.

Ted Stuart had taken Mary on their first date just the weekend before.

"Oh, it's assumed for sure!" responded Mary. "As a matter of fact, we discussed it when we were at Eldridge's looking at engagement rings last weekend. Our biggest problem is whether we will have one kid or two! Not who's asking who out..."

"You mean, whom, darling" interrupted Cindy mockingly as she gazed, trancelike, out the front windshield. There was a short pause and then all three belted out in laughter again. They shared the same English teacher in school who was overly fond of correcting grammar. She had become the most recent target of the girls' derision.

The country side whizzed passed as the car made its way down the highway. Although Kansas City's suburbs were expanding towards Buckner, much of the highway was still lined with desolate pastures until one reached Independence. The hometown of President Harry S. Truman, Independence had two shopping malls. One of them was relatively new and lacked shops while the other, older and more established, was still the "go to" place.

"Do you think the Independence Center will get any more stores in it?" asked Debbie as the car passed the exit with the mall to the right.

Mary glanced quickly to the right to see the big, modern looking shopping center. It seemed so out of place this far from Kansas City. It was as though someone had just plopped it down in the middle of field without regard to the fact that very few people lived out here. It did have a Sears and a Jones Store in it and a few newer boutiques had opened in close proximity to the major stores, but it seemed cavernous and empty right now.

Mary shook her head and replied, "My daddy says the developer was crazy building that out here. He says the people in Independence have more money than sense. I hope it does, though, because it's closer than the Blue Ridge Mall."

"I hope it does, too." Cindy chimed in. "Think of all the stores we could shop in! My daddy says just the opposite about it, though. He thinks more and more people will be moving out this way and building it now while the land is cheap was smart."

The girls continued down the highway discussing the merits of each shopping mall until they came to their exit. Mary carefully veered onto the exit ramp and approached the stoplights that awaited them at the bottom of the hill. She turned left, passing under the overpass and then turned right into the shopping center. As usual, the parking lots were jammed with cars and they drove slowly up and down each aisle looking for an elusive empty parking space. They finally saw one on an opposite parking lane and Mary gunned her car to get to the empty space before someone else beat her to it. Just as they arrived, another car came from the opposite direction and turned on its signal to indicate its claim to the space.

"No way, man!" shouted Debbie. "We were here first!"

Mary was caught between whether to make the right turn into the spot or let the other car have it. Both cars sat frozen waiting for the other to make a concession and leave. The girls looked at each other and began giggling about the situation they found themselves in.

"I guess I'll let him have it." Mary sullenly offered.

"Uh-uh. That's an old man in that car. He can go to the handicap lanes!" laughed Cindy.

"I'll handle this." added Debbie and she jumped out of the car. She casually walked over the other car and the man rolled down his window to talk to her. Mary and Cindy watched with amusement as Debbie displayed her "cute" personality that the boys seemed to love. She and the man talked for a few seconds and then the man turned off his blinker and drove away, smiling and waving to the girls as he passed.

Debbie came back to the car and sat back down in the front seat exclaiming, "Your spot, Mary!"

Mary and Cindy looked at Debbie in amazement and both of them shouted as Mary turned into the spot, "What did you say to him?"

Debbie started laughing so hard she couldn't talk. Both girls started laughing along with her which only seem to make Debbie laugh harder. Then she started pointing at Cindy and nearly choked from whatever was tickling her so. Cindy, looking wide-eyed at Debbie realized that the joke must be on her started insisting, "What did you say?"

Debbie laughed even harder and then took several deep breaths as she try to explain what had just occurred.

"I told him the truth!" she belted out and began laughing again. After one more short blast she settled down enough to finish the story.

"I told him that you were my sister and that you're mentally retarded. If we didn't hurry up and park in this spot, you were gonna wet your pants!"

Debbie and Mary both started laughing again while Cindy sat staring at Debbie.

"You told him I'm an M. R.?" she said acting offended but with a slight lilt in her voice that gave away her lack of earnestness. All three girls started laughing some more as they pulled their purses from the back seat, Mary and Debbie making sure to playfully bonk Cindy on the head with theirs as they swiveled in the seat. They exited the car and quickly walked across the parking lot and entered the shopping mall.

The afternoon was filled with going from store to store and looking at dresses. All three eventually found the perfect dress and they decided it was time to head home. Mary's father was adamant about her being back in Buckner before dark and the afternoon sun was quickly fading. Dusk was upon them when they finally reached the car.

"Man, my Daddy's gonna kill me for being out late." whined Mary.

"Tell him it was my fault, Mary." Cindy quickly replied. "He thinks I'm retarded, too!"

"Everyone thinks you're a dork, Cindy." said Mary. "And that's not a good enough reason to be late."

Mary started up the car and moved it from the parking space. They wound their way through the parking lots and merged into the heavy traffic surrounding the mall's exit. Although Mary was an experienced driver, she was not used to driving in heavy traffic, nor after dark. Her head swiveling from side to side, and mirror to mirror, she avoided cars and finally arrived in the lane that would merge them back onto the highway. Feeling that she could let her guard down and relax a little, Mary began accelerating to match the speeds of the cars on the highway. Unbeknownst to Mary, a semi-truck had failed to turn on its headlights and was in the lane that Mary was about to merge into. Busy talking to Cindy and Debbie, and not seeing the truck in her mirror, she quickly moved directly into the truck's path.

The truck driver saw Mary make her move through his passenger door's lower window; he hit his brakes and quickly turned the truck into the next lane. In doing so, he lost control of the truck causing it to swerve and then jack knife as it skidded to a halt down the center of the highway. Although the left lane had been empty when the truck had started the avoidance maneuver, a car had come up quickly and slammed into the cab of the truck as both vehicles came to a halt.

Mary had barely seen the truck in time to quickly jerk her car to the right and avoid hitting it. Her car bumped down the shoulder of the highway striking two reflector posts that had stood there, knocking them down with loud cracks. She quickly stopped the car and watched as the car smashed into the truck. The three girls were horrified at what they were witnessing as the terror of the moment sunk in. None of them were wearing seatbelts and yet they were unscathed in what could have been a deadly accident for them. All traffic on the highway came to an immediate halt and the driver of the truck quickly got out of his cab and checked on the driver of the car that had hit him. By the time he had gotten there, a man exited the driver's side of his car and met the truck driver at the back of his car. Mary couldn't see the blood on his face but from what she could tell both drivers were okay. They talked to each other for a moment and pointed at Mary's car several times before making their way over to check on her. She and her two friends got out of the car and went to inspect the frontend for damage. The two men met them there and they all discussed what had just happened, relieved that nobody was seriously injured. The driver of the car had broken his nose on the steering wheel of his car, but otherwise he said he was fine.

A Police Cruiser had been canvassing the mall parking lot and the officer inside heard the accident and quickly appeared on the scene. He exited his vehicle and approached the small group standing at the front of Mary's car. His first concern was the safety of the group so he asked them to join him back at his car. He then called his dispatcher to get tow trucks on the scene. A second police cruiser quickly showed up and the officer in it got out and began setting flares on the highway to direct traffic around the accident. He then took position at the first flare and began slowly waving traffic past the scene.

Mary, Cindy and Debbie looked on in shock. What had been a wonderful and fun afternoon had suddenly turned into a nightmare. The police officer took each driver to the back of his car and asked for their version of the accident. He took Cindy's and Debbie's statement, as well. After about thirty minutes, he was done with the interviews and gathered the drivers to talk to them as group. He had determined that the truck driver had be negligent for not using his headlights after dark and issued him a citation. Mary was given the truck driver's insurance information and was asked if her car could run. She thought so, but the officer walked with the girls and opened the hood to look at the engine compartment. He had Mary start the engine, and after watching it run for a few minutes, assured Mary that everything seemed to be okay.

Mary and her two friends entered the car, Mary and Debbie in the front seat, and Cindy in the back, and all three buckled their seatbelts. They were allowed to merge into the slow moving traffic and within a few moments were away from the accident. The drive home was quiet, each girl pondering the possibilities of what could have occurred just a few moments earlier. Mary didn't come close to approaching the speed limit and by the time they reached Buckner, her arms and hands ached from the tight grip she'd maintained on the steering wheel.

Mary dropped the two girls off at their respective houses and proceeded to drive home. Thinking of her friends and how much they meant to her, Mary began to consider how valuable and serious life could be. She decided that it might be important to grow up now and start living her life with meaning; not simply going through the motions of taking each day as it comes. This train of thought led her down a path that ended with Ted. She and Ted had a very nice time together on their date the previous weekend and she was looking forward to going with him to the dance. They had made the arrangements at the end of their evening together so there was no anticipation of rejection that the other two girls were experiencing.

Mary liked Ted. Like all the boys in the school, she had known him most her life but for some reason he seemed different now. He looked more like a man than a boy and seemed more serious. The rest of the boys their age were still into drinking and pulling pranks but Ted seemed to have moved past this. Although he wasn't the smartest student in their class, he studied hard and made good grades. In short, he was a good guy and Mary thought he might be the one for her. She let out a big sigh as she pulled into her driveway, relieved to have made it home safely and pleased with her newfound commitment to life.

Chapter 5

"Conscience is the only clue that will eternally guide a man clear of all doubts and inconsistencies." —Thomas Jefferson

Eighteen months prior to Mary's admittance into Northern Oaks, a Bill sitting on the desk of Governor T. Beauregard Thomas of Mississippi was by far the most difficult one he could ever imagine signing. Tabbed the "Death with Dignity Law" by the press, it had far reaching implications. In its simplest form, the law would give certain individuals living in the State of Mississippi the right to physician-assisted suicide. At its philosophical core, however, the law would legalize murder.

Governor Thomas had always been a devout Christian. He went to worship services regularly; partly to convey that his constituency could trust him and partly to cleanse his soul of the dirtiness he sometimes felt necessary in performing public service. His Sunday mornings spent in church always left him feeling better than he did going in. He definitely had a strong faith, if indeed, he didn't always show it. But this Bill sitting on his desk seemed to question everything he believed in as a Christian. With one stroke of his pen, he would be playing God with Mississippians' lives.

Of course, he was being far more dramatic than the situation before him warranted as a similar law already existed in the State of Washington. Additionally, he did not write the Bill, the State Legislature did. He also never spoke in favor of it, trusting his political instincts that the law would not need his support to come to fruition. Even if he chose to veto the Bill, the Legislature would overturn it and enact the law without him causing him to look politically toothless. Why be politically linked to it? However, the cold reality of the situation was that Mississippi simply didn't have the money to sustain "end-of-life" lives of people who didn't want to live. Governor Thomas was not oblivious as to what was at stake for society.

A perplexing dilemma had been slowly stirring in America since the late 1990's. As medical advances extended life and baby boomers began reaching their senior years, the number of aged individuals relying on the healthcare system to sustain them was growing larger than the number of people from whom the financial support could be had. Economists had been warning America for decades that this situation was coming and it roared down the tracks of inevitability, ignored by an apathetic general populace unwilling to discuss it. How ironic it seemed to the Governor. Here we are at the pinnacle of human achievement in how it relates to extending life and we can't afford to take advantage of it. Mississippi had the bad luck of being one of the poorest States in the Union in income earned per capita, as well as, having one of the most reliant population on the State's Medicaid system. In short, it had the loathsome distinction of being one of the few States in America forced to deal with the problem in this manner.

The "Death with Dignity Law" allowed anyone with a terminal or progressive disease the opportunity to choose death rather than suffer days, weeks, or even years due to their disease state. It had many safeguards built into it in an effort to protect citizens from themselves and the State. While not specific to a diagnosis, the process could only begin when a physician certified that a patient's situation would result in continuing morbidity and eventual death. It did not specify a length of time before the expected death, which concerned the Governor. In his mind, we are all ambling towards death's door and many of the diseases that will thrust us there already exist in us. This seemed like an open invitation for those of lesser illnesses seeking their own premature demise. The medical review board that must give its permission to the suicide request, however, offset this caveat. Additionally, a Psychiatrist's evaluation and certification that the petitioner was of sane mind and poor physical condition was necessary. And most importantly to the Governor, and anyone who resided in the State, under no conditions could euthanasia be directed against anyone other than the petitioner.

In other words, there would be no famed "death panels" determining the future of citizens. Overall, the Governor thought, this law did a good job of mitigating any concern of a State's lackadaisical attitude toward life as any he could think of.

But a philosophical question was born out of the law that Governor Thomas simply didn't have the education or training to address. Even experts in the fields of philosophy and ethics were at odds over the debate. The question arose and had to be answered, "what is the distinction between 'life' and 'living'?" This task would be set before the medical review boards in determining who should be allowed to die. There was and never will be a finite list of qualifications or determinates that can easily be checked off in a review process. Every individual's needs and circumstances will be different and there are bound to be borderline situations that would tax the most pragmatic of thinkers. In the end, it was decided that the determination is simply made by the individual. The responsibility of convincing the medical review board beyond the obvious medical data that one's quality of life is worthless falls directly on the person making the request for assisted suicide.

As if the issue itself wasn't complicated enough, the eyes of the nation were upon Mississippi. The media coverage of the Bill had been exhausting. From cable news outlets to national magazines, the constant media buzz surrounding the capitol droned as loudly as summer cicadas. Politicians could barely leave a building before a reporter would pounce upon them demanding to know what they believed in and where the Bill stood. There was no right answer in dealing with them. If one was naive enough to answer their first question thinking that media exposure was good for a political career, he or she quickly found himself or herself backed into a corner trying to defend the Bill's intent. Many supporters of the legislation were branded "murderers" by the extreme media while others deemed lazy or greedy for not finding better government financed alternatives to improve the quality of life for aging seniors. It was easier and best for the legislators to avoid the reporters and ignore their questions when they couldn't.

With all this fluttering in his mind, Governor Thomas put ink to paper thus finalizing the new law. He knew that the State wouldn't have to wait long for someone to petition the right for assisted suicide and he also knew the State wouldn't have to wait long for some crack pot human rights group to file lawsuits trying to stop the law. One thing he never understood about such groups was their pompous attitude towards the ignorant and stupid masses they purported to help. It was as if they were born with a special knowledge and understanding of how to save humankind from itself. Of course, they weren't too concerned about an individual's rights in the course of protecting human rights. For theirs is a logic of the whole, not the one. Regardless of their efforts, the law will stand. The Constitutionality of it was unquestioned. The morality? Well, that was for future generations to decide.

Chapter 6

"The moving finger writes, and having written moves on. Nor all thy piety nor all thy wit, can cancel half a line of it." —Omar Khayyam

Matitha pushed Mary's wheelchair up to the dining room table as closely as it would go. Because of the overall size of the chair and the armrests that protruded forward, Mary's torso remained a fair distance from the table. This would be problematic for her if she were in any condition to feed herself. Undoubtedly, a portion of every morsel she would have moved to her mouth would have fallen into her lap. But like all other simple tasks now, Mary had lost the ability to lift a fork or spoon and transfer it to her mouth. Shortly after Matitha left, an aide came to her side and asked her what she wanted for breakfast. This was a new aide that Mary hadn't seen before which, of course, wasn't unusual. The aides came and went in places like this and it seemed that the good ones were gone faster than the bad ones.

"What's your name?" asked Mary instead of ordering breakfast.

"I'm Tabitha. I'm new here. I suppose I should've introduced myself." replied the aide.

"Yes, you should have." Mary said agitatedly. Why don't youngsters know any manners these days, thought Mary. But Mary remembered that nursing homes probably didn't get the cream of the crop when it came to healthcare workers. The low pay and dealing with curmudgeons like her wasn't a great enticement for the best and the brightest.

Tabitha looked like a young girl, possibly 18 or 19 years old. She had a tattoo of a dragon on her left arm that stretched the entire length of her pale, lithe forearm. She appeared to be a nail biter, which always concerned Mary about the people who handled her food. She was very thin, almost willowy in appearance.

"You're a skinny little thing, Tabitha. Maybe you should eat my breakfast!" Mary said in an effort to put the girl at ease. "How much change do you keep in your pocket to keep you from blowing away?"

Tabitha smiled and replied, "That's funny. I haven't heard that one before. I get skinny jokes all the time. I don't have much appetite so I don't eat as much as I probably should. Maybe that's why they hired me to work in the Dining Hall." giggled Tabitha.

Mary chuckled at Tabitha's ironic observation and was getting ready to reply when another resident shouted at Tabitha from the next table over, demanding that she come help her right away. Mary thought most of the residents in this facility were extremely rude. They seemed to think that their needs and problems were more important than anyone else's. Some of them would simply shout without even looking at whom they were shouting at as though the aides could pop in and out like magic when summoned. Tabitha excused herself for a moment to take care of the loud woman. She will eventually learn to ignore these sudden outbursts for help, thought Mary, otherwise she will never get anything finished. Cries for assistance were like steady rain around here. With Tabitha off to help someone else, Mary was left alone with her thoughts.

****

The thunder rolled and the sky was darkening at a very quick pace. It was May of 1975 and Mary and her husband, Ted Stuart, had just driven past the Louisiana state line heading into Mississippi. It was a very long drive from Kansas City to Vicksburg and the threat of thunderstorms only heightened the stress in the car. Their '73 Ford Maverick had well-worn tires and easily hydroplaned on wet surfaces. Additionally, they were pulling a small U-Haul trailer that contained everything they owed, paltry as it may be. The combination of heavy wind and constant fishtailing of the trailer had made the drive from Kansas City feel like one of those Automotive Endurance Races that car manufacturers compete in. But unlike the drivers in those races, Mary and Ted were in no hurry to get to where they were going.

The job market in Kansas City had been terrible since Ted and Mary were married a year earlier and Ted had recently accepted a job in Vicksburg working for an oil company. Leaving their friends and family behind was a very difficult decision and one the young couple didn't make hastily. But after many hours of deliberation they both came to the conclusion that a job with a petroleum company offered a bright future given the recent OPEC oil embargo and new emphasis being placed on rebuilding America's energy infrastructure.

So the combination of steady work at decent wages plus helping the country through difficult energy times made the move far more palatable than it normally would have been for the Stuarts. The oil fields in southwestern Mississippi were in desperate need of good mechanics to maintain them and someone like Ted, who had a Vocational Technology degree in engine and pump repair was in high demand. Working out of Vicksburg, Ted would travel the southwest corner of Mississippi on a routine maintenance schedule while being available to travel to any site in the South on an emergency basis. He would not be home much during the workweek but that was the price they were both willing to pay for a good job and a promising future.

As they crossed the State line, Mary sighed knowing that their destination was near. The combination of excitement from the unknown mixed with the dread of starting over left both edgy. It wouldn't take much spark to ignite an argument in the car.

"How much longer til we get there?" asked Mary tentatively, already knowing the answer.

Agitated because he guessed Mary knew the answer, he answered tersely.

"What difference does it make? We'll be there soon enough."

And with that, Mary's attempt at conversation was over. She sullenly looked out the passenger side window and watched as the landscape passed by. The drive through Arkansas had been picturesque with its rolling, wooded hills. Very few homes could be seen from the highway and she wondered if anyone lived in the State outside of the cities. Occasionally, she would spot a cabin or small home situated deep in the woods which set her mind wondering what kind of people lived in such isolated areas. Although she hailed from a small town herself, her family lived in town not far from the big city of Kansas City, so she had no basis for comparison. She thought of TV shows like the Beverly Hillbilly's, or Petty Coat Junction which portrayed these people as unsophisticated hicks. But she doubted that they were really that silly and backwards.

As they travelled into Louisiana, the hills gave way to flatter landscape with even more trees. In fact, although she didn't know what to expect, Mary was surprised at all the tall pine trees that lined the highway all the way across Louisiana and into Mississippi. The image reminded her of her childhood picture books of primeval forests. She half expected to see mounted knights in shining armor dart across the highway on their way to some hidden adventure. One thing Mary had always had was an active imagination. That, and very poor radio reception, had kept her occupied during the hours that Ted chose not to talk.

The first year of marriage had been fun but stressful. Ted could be such a loving, gentle man at times. However, marriage had exposed some behaviors in him she did not see before their matrimony. Whether it was the stress from not having consistent work or the added burden of supporting a new lifestyle, Ted would sink into angry moments where he would snipe at Mary, leaving her feeling cold and alone. She didn't regret marrying him; she simply didn't understand what she could do during these times to help him feel better. Apparently, the next few hours in the car was going to be one of those times.

The time passed slowly as the rest of the trip was uneventful. The company that had hired Ted arranged for them to live in an apartment complex for six months until they could find more permanent living quarters. They pulled into the parking lot and came to a stop in front of the leasing office. Both sat quietly and stared out the front windshield. After a brief moment, Ted broke the ice.

"Well, here we are." he said with a sigh in his voice. "I suppose we should go inside and get our key."

Mary hesitated then spoke. "Are you sure this is what we should do? It seems so—so permanent now that we are here."

Ted looked at Mary and smiled wryly, just like her father would do. "Hmmm, this doesn't seem like the time or place to rethink our decision." He chuckled and continued, "I think we made a very good decision and we have a really cool future ahead of us here. Yeah, we're gonna miss our friends and family but we'll make new friends and start our own family."

Mary slowly nodded her head with a distant look in her eyes.

"Besides," he went on, "this will give you the chance to get your teaching degree. I don't know if you would have done that at home with all the distractions."

Mary shook herself out of the trance she had fallen into and turned suddenly to Ted. In a panic she blurted out.

"But that's because I will be so lonely here when you're traveling. I've got to do something! I'm really afraid of being lonely..."

"Mary," he replied in his most tender and loving voice, "you'll never be lonely. Even when I'm not here physically, I'll call you and we'll talk as we always do. And even if we don't talk, I'll always be loving you. Plus, the Mary I know has always been the easiest person to get along with. I suspect you will be leading a neighborhood committee or volunteer organization before you know it. It won't take long for women around here to figure out how wonderful and special you are. "

Mary smiled at Ted and thought, "See? This is why I love this man! He can be so cranky and quiet at times but then he'll turn on a dime and say the most beautiful, loving things to me."

"I suppose you're right. You're always right—except when I'm more right!" she answered with a giggle in her voice. And with that conversation concluded, they found the courage to exit the car and proceed into the office. As they did, she thought to herself, "maybe Mississippi won't be all that bad."

****

Tabitha returned to Mary's table within 5 minutes and proceeded to ask Mary if she had any special requests for her breakfast. Tabitha's supervisor makes all the meal decisions, carefully making sure that every resident in the home gets the proper nutrition and calories that they need while keeping an eye on allergies and other conditions that prevent unsuspecting residents from eating certain foods. With that understanding, the meals at this nursing home, and most others, were at best bland and at times nearly inedible in Mary's opinion.

"What's the pie today, Tabitha?" Mary asked with amusement.

"Pie? It's breakfast time!" was Tabitha's inquisitive reply.

"Yes, I said 'pie.'"

Tabitha frowned. She had heard that many residents in the facility had memory and comprehension issues but she didn't think Ms. Stuart was supposed to be one of them.

She cautiously said, "The pie, for lunch, is Chocolate Cream or Apple Pie. But that's dessert for lunch. Do you want anything special for breakfast?"

"Tabitha, are you aware that today is my last day here?"

Tabitha nodded her head slowly, now fully understanding where the conversation was headed.

"Then let me ask you. If it was your last meal what would you eat? Flavorless bacon and eggs or Chocolate Cream Pie?"

Tabitha simply nodded her head for she didn't want to state the obvious. She knew Mary was right and why not indulge her? For that matter, why should she be limited to one piece of pie? However, this was her first day on the job and she doubted whether she should be promising anything she couldn't deliver. Throwing caution to the wind, as was her nature, Tabitha wanted to make this day special for Mary. She robustly exclaimed,

"Mary, you're absolutely right! I asked you what you wanted and if it's pie, by gosh, it will be pie! Now the next question is, how many pieces?"

She and Mary both chuckled and Mary concluded. "I think I will start with two and see from there. Thank you, Tabitha."

And with a smile on her face, Tabitha briskly headed to the kitchen to get Mary's breakfast.

****

Not far from where Mary was dining, Matitha was hunting for a priest. She knew Father Stewart was in the facility somewhere, as this was the day he made his rounds in the nursing center. Matitha had known Father Stewart for several years and he seemed as much a fixture in Northern Oaks as the furniture. Of course, many men of religion came through the nursing home. Whether they be ministers to specific patients, or ministers that made rounds to many nursing homes like Father Stewart, they were frequent visitors. One busy day in particular, Matitha and her fellow nurses joked that there more preachers in the home than residents. The staff concluded that there must be a whole lot of sinnin' going on in Northern Oaks for God to call down such a plague!

After searching all the corridors in both A and C wings, she finally found the priest leaving a resident's room in B wing. He was wearing his usual clerical clothing and exhibiting his trademark smile and good looks. Like most of the staff at Northern Oaks, Matitha liked Father

Stewart. He had a certain casualness about his demeanor that instantly put one at ease. It didn't hurt that he was young, very fit, with sandy blonde hair and blue eyes. Many of the nurses thought his celibacy was a waste of dashing good looks. For his part, Father Stewart was deeply devout and didn't miss, nor desire, a relationship other than the one he shared with God.

Seeing Matitha approaching him, Father Stewart stopped and waited to see if she was seeking him. She smiled as she approached him and he nodded with a succinct bow of his head and said,

"Hello, Matitha. How are you doing today?"

Matitha, slightly out of breath from her efforts to locate him responded, "Father Stewart. I'm so glad I's found you. I must of searched everywhere's for you. I'm fine, thank you and how are you today?"

"I'm very well, thank you." he said pleasantly. "Sorry to be such an inconvenience. What can I help you with?"

Matitha cut her eyes sideways as if searching for the right words to explain her request. After a moment's pause, she replied to the priest.

"Father Stewart, I have a very big favor to asks of you. I don't know if you will do it and I don't blames you if you won't, but it never hurts to ask, right?"

Intrigued where Matitha was going with this, he chuckled, "Of course not! I'm here to be of service. So what is it, Matitha?"

"Well," she continued, "You probably don't know Mary Stuart, do ya? She's a Baptist so there's no reason for you to. But I's wondering if you would have time to talk to her before you leave today?"

"Mary Stuart, you say?" replied the priest. "Her name doesn't ring a bell other than the obvious. I don't suppose she's kin to me, is she?"

Matitha snickered in her breathy way. She hadn't even considered that they shared the same last name.

"Oh no, Father Stewart. Her Stuart is spelled differently than yours. But wouldn't that be funny what with her being Baptist and all... Perhaps when you talks to her, you should bring that up!"

Matching Matitha's amusement, Father Stewart chortled, "You're right, Matitha. That might be a good way to put her at ease. But why do you want me to talk to her?"

Matitha paused again, considering her words carefully.

"Well, Mama is scheduled for euthanasia this afternoon and I don't blame her for wantin' to go and all, but I believe that she still has good days left in her. I've talked to her til's I's blue in the face but can't seem to change her mind. I thought you might have better luck with her. Everyone likes you so much around here and I'm sure Mama would too. She's so sweet. I'm sure she'd listen to you."

Father Stewart's interest peaked and he gazed deeply at Matitha when he heard her refer to Mary as, "mama."

"You called her, Mama, Matitha. Was that by accident?"

"Oh no, Father Stewart." she said shaking her head forcefully from side to side. "I didn't make a mistake. I's called her Mama almost since I met her because she reminds me so much of my own Mama."

It was Father Stewart's turn to pause and think about the matter for a moment. Matitha's request was very unusual and he was sure she knew better than to be making it. But she clearly held Mary in very high esteem or she wouldn't be going to such lengths to save her. He also knew Matitha was a very passionate nurse who cared deeply for her patients but he doubted that she referred to many of them as family. This was a very interesting situation to find himself in.

"Matitha, it really isn't my place to minister to anyone who doesn't request it from me. Mary is entitled to her privacy. Additionally, there's no guarantee she would even listen if we did talk. Don't you think it may be a bit rash?"

Matitha was shaking her head back and forth throughout the priest's assertion.

"No, I don't Father." replied Matitha. "I know one thing for certain. I'd do anything I can before I's let someone close to me die. Mary is like a mother to me and I'm gonna fight to change her mind as long as I can! And if you don't wanna help, I'll find someone else who can!"

Father Stewart was momentarily stunned by Matitha's resolve. Mary must be quite a woman for Matitha to feel this way. It sounded like his life would be blessed if he got to know her before her passing. With that in mind and the attitude that he would merely visit with Mary, not press her about her decision; he decided to accept Matitha's invitation to talk with Mary.

"Matitha, if it means this much to you, I will meet Mary and talk with her a little bit. I won't try to change her mind, but I will give her my thoughts if the conversation comes up. Is that acceptable to you?"

Matitha's face broke out in a huge grin and she nearly jumped in the air in her excitement.

"Oh yes, Father. Thank you so much. I just know you will make a difference. You're so wonderful! You just wait here while I go figure out where Mama is. I'll be back and gets ya soon."

Matitha spun on her heels and headed down the hall at a very quick pace. Father Stewart watched her go and marveled at the depth of her concern. Death was such a common event in nursing homes that one would think that staff would just accept it and move on. But from his travels through this home and many others like it, he'd determined that, despite the violence and killing that the media daily reported, humanity, for the most part, valued life—even feeble life with very little left to live for.

He decided to wait at the end of the hall next to an emergency exit door so that he would be out of the way of the nurses and aides who were bustling from room to room. Looking out the window that filled the top half of the door, he began to think about the Death with Dignity Law that Mississippi had adopted. He had conflicted feelings about it.

As a Catholic priest, he was beholden to the Tenets that the Church attested to in its canons. There was no doubt or speculation where the Church stood on life and death, and specifically suicide. In the recently revised Catechism of the Catholic Church, the Church condemned absolutely "an act or omission which, of itself or by intention, causes death in order to eliminate suffering" However, there are certain exceptions to the rule that cloud the picture somewhat. For instance, we are not obligated to use disproportionate means to maintain life; means that do not offer us a reasonable hope of benefit or impose on us an excessive burden. If Mary were to go into cardiac arrest, she mostly likely has a DNR on file that prohibited her resuscitation and medical staff and clergy accept this course of action. In light of her age and overall health, it would be illogical to deny her a "natural" death due to the burden it would impose both physically and financially on Mary. But a gray area is drawn when one tries to objectively define words like, "disproportionate" and "excessive burden".

"Who is to say what is and isn't disproportionate?" thought Father Stewart. "Given Mary's situation, is her care disproportionate to her overall existence? Is she experiencing excessive burden?" In other words, what IS the price tag, both financially and spiritually, we place on Mary's life? While Father Stewart had shown great interest studying Philosophy in Seminary, the more he examined it, the more he realized that it just opened more doors and questions that had no definable answers. The circular pursuit of it all convinced him that it was foolhardy to try to address questions of life that have no answers. That is what Faith is for, he decided, and that is where he would rest his soul.

Still gazing out the window but seeing nothing due to the depth of his thinking, Father Stewart made the decision that Faith was the only answer to this question. For thousands of years, the Catholic Church has provided the framework for living and dying, and it was delivered upon the message of Faith. Subsequently it would be wrong of him to detour from the Church's teaching without cause. To that end, Father

Stewart decided to investigate Mary's medical situation and depending upon what he found there, find a way to convince her that she was making a mistake.

The decision made, he quickly strolled down the corridor to the nurse's station at the other end. He left a message at the station to send Matitha to the Head Nurse's office to find him. Feeling it was extremely important to know more about Mary, he hurried off relieved that Divine guidance lay somewhere in the facts of the situation.

Chapter 7

"There is nothing unpremeditated, nothing neglected by God. His unsleeping eye beholds all things." —Saint Basil

After Tabitha had fed Mary every morsel of the two pieces of Chocolate Pie, she called for an aide to come get Mary. Mary sat quietly as she waited watching the other residents finish their breakfasts. Some of the tables were occupied by residents that neither spoke nor looked around. They simply munched the food inserted into their mouths while their heads bowed down never raising their gaze from their laps. How pathetic, she thought. Other than the constant pain that plagued her, her condition seemed far less serious than theirs. She wondered why they don't let go of life and head to a brighter future? Other residents were talking and seemed to be having a nice time. The contrast was amazing to Mary. The degree of human condition in this place swung dramatically. There were people that one would question why they would reside here in the first place to people that seemed frail shells of human nothingness. "How do they see me in this equation?" she wondered.

What she did know, however, was that Northern Oaks was a privately funded nursing home and that the people who resided here paid for the quality of life they received. For that, they were given as good of care as possible for the money they paid. She knew this would not be the case in a facility funded by the State's Medicaid dollars. The Medicaid funded facilities operated at a fraction of the privately supported facilities. For every dollar Northern Oaks received to provide care, a Medicaid facility would receive approximately twenty five cents.

This translated to the obvious. The Medicaid facilities were old buildings in poorer parts of town. They were kept clean but not well maintained. They seemed dark and institutional compared to Northern Oaks. Because of a Medicaid facility's location and lower pay scales, the healthcare workers were the worst educated and trained. Additionally, the residents there were either poor to begin with or had outlived their resources, as Mary had done, so they were in far worst physical condition as a whole than the residents at Northern Oaks. She shuddered to think that this would be the next stop through life. She did not want to spend her final years in such comparably horrible conditions.

The aide arrived at her table and asked pleasantly, "Where to, Ms. Stuart?"

"I think I'll have you park me by the aviary, if that's not already taken. And when we get there, can you please tilt my chair back? My back and legs are really hurting."

"Of course, Ms. Stuart. Glad to do it." he said and began pushing her from the dining hall.

He briskly wheeled her to the front of the facility where the aviary was located. As they went down a long hall, they stopped to make room for an ambulance crew. The crew didn't seem to be in a hurry so that meant one of two things to Mary. Either the resident they were after had already died or they were there to retrieve one for tests or care at a hospital. Mary had once tried to calculate what it cost to take a resident to the hospital. She had never had to go to the hospital since arriving here so she didn't really have a good idea. She figured the ambulance ride was several thousand dollars and depending on the length of stay, she thought the hospital stay would run around five thousand dollars or more a day. What a waste of resources she thought for some of these residents that everyone knew wouldn't live much longer. Of course, what was the alternative for those who treasured life? Mary didn't have an answer. She only knew that in her case she had done all she could to not drain the healthcare system anymore. She had signed a DNR, or "Do Not Resuscitate", directive forbidding healthcare workers from reviving her in the event she suffered cardiac arrest. What a blessing it would have been for her to have passed quietly rather than make the decision she had made.

Once they turned the corner of the long hall, they were in a Nurse Station area. A Nurse Station was at the center of the hub and resident halls flared away from the station in every direction. This allowed nurses to quickly access a lot of rooms and manage the residents more efficiently. However, in a facility the size of Northern Oaks which had multiple hubs connected to various other halls, the effect on outside visitors was confusing and resulted in many getting lost in the labyrinth of similar looking hallways and rooms. Of course, Mary's aide knew where he was going and they found the aviary unattended allowing Mary to parked directly in front of it for her viewing pleasure.

The aide pulled her up to it and swung her feet towards the aviary so that she was looking directly at it. He was getting ready to leave when Mary reminded him that he needed to tilt the wheelchair to alleviate her pain. He apologized and tilted the seat back. Unfortunately, this left Mary's lap and legs between her and the aviary, blocking her view. He noticed this and swung the wheelchair around so the she could turn her head slightly to the right to see the birds. He asked her if she needed anything else. She shook her head no and he hurriedly went on his way.

Mary loved watching the birds flit back and forth in the large glass box. There were small nests built into the wall opposite the front glass. The nests were all occupied by finches of various colors and markings. She suspected there were eggs in some of the nests as one of the aides had told her a separate company manages the aviary and removes baby birds from time to time. But she was in no position to see them if there were any. The aviary reminded her of Springtime and all the birds that seemed to appear out of nowhere back in Buckner. Winter was so desolate and bleak in Northern Missouri but once Spring took hold, life suddenly reappeared. The birds were always the first sign that better days lay ahead.

****

The news was sad and shocking. Mary couldn't have any children. The Ultra Sound taken of her pelvis revealed that her left ovary had never formed and the right one was only partially formed. Although it probably functioned normally, the doctors suspected it didn't produce any viable eggs. Mary and Ted were crushed by the news. Part of the certainty that the move to Vicksburg was a good decision was predicated on starting a family in Mississippi. This news was the first setback they had encountered since moving six years earlier.

Since the move, Mary had completed a four year degree in Primary Education from Alcorn State University and had just finished her first year as a First Grade Teacher at Beechwood Elementary School located in the heart of Vicksburg. She loved working with the children and quickly became one of the favorite teachers in the school. She actively participated in the PTA and volunteered to stay after school to tutor students of all ages in need of help. Her commitment to education was very strong but her willingness to be out of the house when Ted was away working was equally driving. His work had recently demanded that he be gone at least four days a week, and many times five. While Mary had made some very good friends in school and her neighborhood, nothing really took the place of his absence as teaching had. It consumed her during the week and gave the happy couple much to talk about when Ted returned for the weekends.

But this setback was crushing. She broke down in tears and poured out to Ted in a moment of sobbing anguish he had never experienced before. She felt like they had lost a child already born into the world, not simply the potential. Forever the optimist, Ted held her and reassured her that it would be okay.

"Oh Mary," he softly spoke trying to soothe her as he gently and lovingly rocked her in his arms, "this doesn't mean anything for certain. The doctors said there is a still an outside chance we can have a baby."

Mary only convulsed harder. She felt as though the very fabric of her soul had been shorn in two and there would be no recovery. The more she visualized the newborn baby she would never hold, the more the mental image gripped and wrested her composure. It was as though a diabolical demon had possessed her that kept flashing images of cooing infants and bouquets of baby powder into her conscious unwilling to release her until he had thoroughly destroyed her. Even after a dam breaks though, gravity eventually has nothing left to push out and so it was with Mary's heartbreak and weeping. As her tears subsided, she laid her head on Ted's shoulder and stared with glassy red eyes at the floor. She gasped a final shudder of emotion as she went totally limp in his arms.

Strongly, Ted held her for what felt likes hours. There were no words to be said or thoughts to convey that would soften the moment. The unforeseen and callous future had been laid before them and all the sorrow in the world couldn't undo it. Ted gently stroked her head, following her hair down her back. When he reached the end, he began again. Over and over he held her and caressed her until the light began to fade from the day. Finally, he spoke.

"I love you, Mary."

And with those words, Mary began to softly cry again.

The next day, Mary woke up feeling somewhat better. Through a restless night, she had awoken many times with spurts of emotional fits denying the bad news. These fits eventually subsided into logical reasoning that perhaps the doctors were wrong and there was a chance she and Ted could have their own baby. Until then, she dedicated her life to her "children" that she taught at school. They would receive her full love and attention. For now, she and Ted decided to go buy her a canary to keep her company when she was home alone. While a dog or cat might have made a better companion, she wanted a bird that would remind her, like a beautiful baby she could call her own, what beauty lies so close yet can't be held.

Chapter 8

"Is freedom anything else than the right to live as we wish?" —Epictetus
As Mary enjoyed the birds in the aviary, she began to regret not having taken any pain medication. The pain in her joints and back radiated through her body and even with her chair in a tilted back position, she was experiencing spasms that were beginning to make her nauseous. She tried to reposition herself but with lack of strength and dexterity, she was rewarded with very little movement. Just when she was arriving at the point of requesting help, Matitha appeared in her peripheral vision and exclaimed,

"I knew I'd find you here! Mama do love them birds."

Mary turned her head to get a better view of Matitha and in doing so, noticed she wasn't alone. Her pain was so awful, though, she didn't have time to remark on the visitor but tore straight to the point with Matitha.

"Oh Matitha. I'm so glad you're here. You were right about not taking my meds this morning. I'm in such pain right now that I want you to drug me up right away. Please go get me something to take the edge off. But don't make it so strong that it clouds my judgment."

Hearing this set Matitha into her bull mode. When Matitha saw something she didn't like, she would set her face stern and it appeared that every muscle in her body flexed and she became two sizes bigger.

"Mama, I knew I shouldn't had listened to you. You's always thinkin' you knows more than everyone else what's good for you! But before I go, this is Father Stewart. He was looking for you. It'nt it funny? He has the same last name as you. Now, you two can talk while I go gets your pain meds."

And with that, Matitha was off like a shot. Lord help anyone who tried to stop her when she was on a mission such as this. Mary often wondered where Matitha had been her whole life. With a friend like her, nothing bad would have ever touched Mary.

The sudden absence of Matitha gave the priest the opportunity to introduce himself and the reason he was seeking Mary.

"Hello Mary. Matitha is a fine nurse. I don't believe I've known any better. As she said, I'm Father Stewart and I was, indeed, looking for you."

"Hello Father." Mary responded suspiciously. "It's nice to meet you but I'm sure you're aware that I'm not Catholic."

The priest nodded his head appreciatively and replied, "I know Mary, but in times such as these God's love favors no denomination. I make rounds here to see my Catholic flock everyday and being aware that you were scheduled for euthanasia today, I wanted to make sure your soul was attended to."

Offended, Mary stared at the priest and the boldness of his suggestion that her soul was unprepared. Of course it was prepared! Didn't he know she was and had always been as one with Christ? But, of course, he did not know anything about Mary other than she was not part of his "flock", as he had put it.

"I appreciate you concern, Father, but I have prayed devotedly about this decision and will spend time with the nursing home's chaplain this afternoon before I go in." Mary said in her most dignified voice.

The priest smiled and appeared at ease with her reply. "Well then," he replied, "do you mind if I spend a few moments with you talking about your decision? As you're probably aware, the Catholic Church has taken a very strong stance against the course of action you have chosen. As a priest in the church, it would be wrong to suggest that I believe otherwise. However, because of my closeness to this nursing home and others in the community, I might see things slightly differently than those who, let's see how should I put this? —call the shots?"

The priest smiled at Mary in such a way that made her feel like she could trust him. She also noticed that he was a nice looking young man and her own intrigue somewhat softened her suspicion of him.

"Are you suggesting then, that you aren't going to try to talk me out of it?" she said wincing as a sudden spasm of pain shot through her back.

"Not at all!" beamed Father Stewart. "I intend to try my best to talk you out of it! I simply said what I did so that you know that regardless of our conversation, I will not judge or think ill of you. Mary, it would take a fool not to see the pain you are in. I'm also aware that you have no family to tend to you and that you would be moved to a State supported facility in less than a week. So, in short. I understand. I don't approve, but I understand."

Agitated again by her immense pain and this nice man's good but misplaced intentions, Mary answered gruffly, "I didn't ask you to come talk to me nor am I seeking your approval. But as you are here and you have been kind, plus the fact that I can't really leave, I will speak with you about my decision."

She again winced as pain struck through her body.

Father Stewart saw the pain in her eyes and his sympathy was further heightened. He loved ministering to the ill and decrepit but the pain he saw at times made him question his own convictions. "Why must people suffer so?" he asked internally. "Why must our existence be defined by such pain and loss?" Of course, he knew the spiritual answers and endeavored to believe in them. But it would be a lie to himself and anyone who asked to say he didn't question God at times like these. He also knew that evil was always present and trying to break the armor of the faithful and that he would never succumb to it. With this mixed bag of feelings, he continued the interview.

"Tell me about your spiritual life, Mary." he said in the truest sense of curiosity.

Mary turned her head back to the birds and watched them flutter back and forth in the confined space they inhabited. She suddenly identified with the birds as she considered her response to the priest. Like the birds, her faith could fit nicely into a spiritual box that allowed her room to move freely but not exit completely. She started talking in a very deliberate voice.

"I was born into a faithful family and attended church service every Sunday at the Baptist church in our town until my husband and I moved to Mississippi. I've always been a devout Christian. As a child, we performed Bible drills in Sunday school until we could almost quote the entire Bible!" she smiled at the recollection. "Of course, I exaggerate but I do know my Bible, as does any good Baptist. It has been my comfort and guide throughout my life. I truly believe that we have everything we need in life written in the Bible. I wish more people knew that..." and her voice trailed off.

"As do I." replied Father Stewart. "I don't believe we do enough with our congregations to open this possibility. A verse or two a week does not have the same kind of rigor that the Bible drills you mentioned do. Have you remained Baptist?"

"Yes. Ted and I found a wonderful church home in Vicksburg and we remained members there until Ted died. I stopped going to church service after that. Not out of spite or anything like that." she said as another burst of flame ignited in her back. Grimacing she continued. "I simply didn't want to be there without him. It hurt too much."

Not sure whether the pain on her face reflected her current physical state or her revelation, Father Stewart asked, "Mary, can I get you anything? A drink of water or move your chair?"

"Yes, Father. Can you tilt this seat to a more upright position? You just squeeze those brake-like thingies and push me up."

Father Stewart was familiar with the wheelchair she was in and had seen many patients moved in the manner Mary requested. He walked behind the chair and began slowly raising her back to a more natural seating position.

"Let me know when to stop, Mary."

"Right there is good, Father. Thank you." she said with a show of relief that indicated the spasms had temporarily subsided.

Father Stewart walked around the wheelchair and picked up a nearby chair for himself. He brought it to the side of Mary's wheelchair and sat down.

After a moment of silence, Mary began again.

"Father. I know you don't like what I'm doing, but I'm confident you can't show me anywhere in the Bible where it says that one can't take one's own life."

The priest was momentarily stunned by such a statement. He quickly gathered himself though and responded.

"On the contrary, Mary. The Fifth Commandment states unequivocally that 'thou shalt not kill'. Jesus instructs us in Matthew to 'put away your sword, for those who live by it shall die by it.' How can you argue that killing yourself is not murder and therefore not a sin?"

"Father, I don't disagree with anything you say but sometimes what is directly said in the Bible doesn't apply to every situation. For instance, we know that the Bible says that there is moral ground to kill in the case of war or self defense. Right?"

"Yes, but this hardly..." but before he could finish, Mary continued.

"And did not Samson commit suicide when he brought down the temple on the Philistines? And then lest we forget the biggest sacrifice of all, Jesus dying on the cross for our sins?"

Flabbergasted at what he just heard, Father Stewart quickly rebutted.

"Mary. What you just said is blasphemy. You should never place yourself on the same level with Christ. Considering your condition, I'm sure God understands better than I why you would say such a thing and He will forgive you. But I caution you not to consider Jesus' surrender to the cross as suicide. So I will not accept that argument. However, your point on Samson and dying for just cause is accurate. How can you justify the taking of your own life as just cause?"

Mary had been contemplating this decision for months and had rationalized her decision nearly as long ago. Her reply was steady and directly to the point.

"Father, I have no one left to share my life with. My family is gone. What few friends I have left must travel distances that they cannot manage to see me. I rely on nurses to feed me, clean me, cloth me and move me. My utility value on earth is exhausted. And even worse, so is my ability to financially support myself. In short, I am unworthy to remain alive. I have nothing to give and I take greatly. It is for the better good that I depart."

The effort it took Mary to say this nearly drained her. Additionally, the pain was already beginning to flare again. Luckily, she heard the unmistakable heel clicks coming down the hall that she knew belonged to Matitha. Relief was close at hand.

The priest contemplated Mary's response for a brief moment and noticed that Matitha's return was imminent. His time with Mary was short.

"Mary, I will not cheapen what you've just told me by falsely stating that I agree. I dedicated my life to the Lord long ago, foregoing any personal ambitions or desires. In doing so, I cherish the opportunity to help people in your state. You are not a drain on society or any of us that feel lucky enough to have the opportunity to serve you. Your desire to no longer be a burden on this planet is noble, but misguided. You forget all the people who find pleasure in helping you and are dedicated to serving your needs. Without you, and others like you, their lives would be less fulfilling." He paused for a moment and looking into Mary's pain filled eyes continued. "I find it interesting that you didn't mention the horrible pain you must endure in your reasoning."

Matitha and the RN that accompanied her came within earshot of the conversation and slowed their pace considerably. While Matitha's urge to quickly administer the pain medication was great, her concern for Mary's soul was greater. They stopped completely about ten feet from the couple.

The timing of the priest's comment couldn't have been better as another nauseating wave of pain was shooting through her body again. Mary waited until it subsided and then responded.

"Father Stewart, it's easier for me to face my decision when thinking of it in the context of helping others. While I think anyone in my situation would jump at the chance to permanently rid themselves of the pain and humility of being totally dependant upon care, I feel less selfish justifying it as a win-win for everyone concerned. Please try to understand how painful and hopeless my life has become. There is no getting better for me. Only more pain or drug induced states of unconscious lethargy. I'm just grateful that I can pursue this course of action."

Father Stewart noticed that Matitha had returned and didn't want to delay the administration of pain medications any longer. In fact, he felt the conversation might have gone better had he waited until she was medicated. It occurred to him at this moment why Mary would have forsaken her medicine today. It must be far easier to finish the deed that awaited her if for no other reason than to escape her immense pain. He took her small forearm into his and made the sign of the cross. He turned to leave and said.

"God made you with all His goodness and love, Mary. You've been a great blessing to many and you will bask in His glory. God bless you, Mary." He gently squeezed her arm then turned and walked away.

Matitha and the RN approached Mary quickly upon hearing the priest's final words.

The nurse pulled the cap from the hypodermic she was carrying and quickly and carefully injected it into Mary's scraggly arm. The morphine quickly rushed through her system and Mary's pain subsided. She weakly smiled up at Matitha who sighed in relief at the effectiveness of the drug. After seeing Mary's apparent relief, the RN turned and headed back to her station.

"That was nice of the priest to come and talk to you, Mama." Matitha said. "I hope it helped you."

Mary sat for a few seconds reflecting on the conversation as her pain eased. She was still confused why the priest had sought her out.

"Matitha, did you put him on me?" asked Mary sternly.

"Why, Mama! You know I wouldn't "put" someone on you." exclaimed Matitha.

Not believing Matitha for a moment, Mary replied.

"Well, I think you did and I appreciate what you were trying to do but it isn't going to work. The conversation with him weakened me and now I feel tired. So, please, I beg of you. Let it go. This is not how I want to spend my final moments."

Matitha's face instantly saddened upon hearing Mary's words. Mary was right. Matitha had sought out the priest to help change Mary's mind. But she didn't want to ruin Mary's last day by causing her more distress. This, coupled with her emotional outbreak earlier in the day, was proving Matitha to be far less than she wanted to be for Mary. She wanted to help Mary, not aggravate her.

"I'm so sorry, Mama. I'm just trying to help but I just keep messin' things up. Well, no more. You just tell Matitha what's you want and I will make it happen!" promised Matitha emphasizing the words, "make it happen".

"Thank you, Matitha. Right now, I just want to be left alone. Please tilt my chair back so I can rest and watch my birds. I'll feel better by lunch time."

Matitha did as she said and then hurried off to see to her other patients, leaving Mary alone with her thoughts.

Chapter 9

"Accept loss forever." —Jack Kerouac

Ted Stuart was a quiet man and enjoyed his time spent driving alone through the back roads of Mississippi. It wasn't that he didn't like people. On the contrary, he was very affable when hanging out with "the boys". But in most conversations, his role was that of commentator and never initiator. Mary liked this about Ted because she was prone to begin discussions and didn't like competing with him when he was in the mood to start talking.

It had been 37 years since he and Mary moved to Vicksburg, and Ted was looking forward to retirement. He had spent his entire career with one company and loving what he did. Because he spent so much time on the road driving from one pump station to another, he knew Mississippi better than any local cartographer. It gave him great comfort to know his job and territory so well. The long drives also gave him plenty of time for introspection and listening to satellite radio. He had grown tired listening to talk radio through the years and now mainly listened to music stations. Occasionally, he would switch over to Comedy channels to lighten his mood.

December weather in Mississippi could change very quickly in the northern portion of the State. What had started the day as a cold rain was rapidly deteriorating into sleet and ice. While no snow was in the forecast, the current conditions were far worse. Driving in snow, his four-wheel drive utility pickup truck could go almost anywhere, but this type of precipitation was far more treacherous. The Traction Control feature on his truck was great for starting under most conditions but did nothing for stopping on slippery surfaces. The best course of action in icy conditions was for Ted to slow his vehicle down and be diligently aware of road conditions. Fortunately, he was nearly to the failing pump station he'd been assigned to repair that day and most of the drive was on gravel roads, which helped neutralize the slipperiness.

Due to the weather, he arrived at the station nearly an hour later than his anticipated arrival time and hurriedly ran from his truck to the small utility shed that sat next to the oil pump. On his way, he noticed that the pump had quit working entirely. This wasn't uncommon as every pump had a shut off switch that interrupted the flow of electricity in the event of mechanical or electrical resistance. This safety feature kept the pump from destroying itself or catching fire in the event of a malfunction. Ted's first job was to reset the switch to make sure that the problem didn't reside in it first.

Upon doing so, he heard a large whine and the switch and pump immediately shut down again. His trained ear told him that the problem wasn't electrical in nature. The whine signified to him that the pump's motor was trying to move the pump but was unable to. "Great..", he thought, "I get to work out in the freezing rain." Unwilling to accept this first test with the thought of working outside, he reset the switch again with the same results.

He left the relative comfort of the shed and began to make his way to the pump that was about 10 yards away. It's large hammer-like counterweight rested just past it's highest arc point as if poised to come down and strike an imaginary anvil. Ted immediately saw the obstruction that was preventing the pump from working properly. A large tree limb had wedged itself between the counterweight and piston on both sides of the pump. Surprised, Ted looked around for the nearest trees and saw that a small grove lay about 100 yards to the southwest. He thought it must have been some wind and incredible happenstance to take a limb this size, hurl it so far, and jam it where it did. He grabbed at the base of the limb in an effort to pull it free from its trappings, but to no avail. He hadn't expected it to budge, but he didn't savor the thought of crawling in amongst the pump's structure with a chainsaw to remove it. After a couple of more tugs, he resigned himself to the necessary task at hand.

He headed back to his vehicle and opened a side panel located in the bed of the truck. He pulled out a fairly large chainsaw and set it on the ground. Even though he always refilled the gas tank on any motor he used when done, he opened the gas lid and checked to make sure the tank was full. He then primed the saw by pressing a small bulb a few times and gave the handle a quick yank. The saw immediately fired to life, puffing out a large ball of smoke that quickly dissipated in the drizzle. He let the loud motor run for a few moments giving it quick little bursts of gas causing it to increase in volume as he did. He then killed the switch and took the chainsaw over to the pump.

Unsure where to start cutting, he stood and stared at the situation for a moment. Realizing that the limb was pinched in two places, he decided to remove the branching end from one side first and work his way back to the opposite side. The saw cut through the smaller limbs with very little effort. He then stepped between the left piston and counterweight's arm and began sawing the main limb. The two inches of wood gave into the chainsaw very quickly leaving just a small piece wedged between two pieces of steel. The freezing rain was beginning to pick up in intensity and Ted was growing slightly impatient with the task. He quickly moved to the other side of the pump and began cutting the limb. With the limb nearly severed, the pump suddenly sprang into motion. The hammer began dropping creating a scissor effect between the beam of the counterweight and the piston mounts. Surprised and alarmed that the pump had begun working despite the safety switch being off, Ted tried to move quickly from the impending danger. However, the icy conditions made his footing treacherous and he fell directly into the path of the falling counterweight. His head and chest where crushed and Ted was instantly killed.

Nearly simultaneously and several hundred miles away, Mary arrived home from her day of teaching school. She was in a wonderful mood as the Elementary School had ended the school day with every class having a Holiday Party. Her Second Graders fully understood what a Holiday Party was, despite the school district's efforts to be politically correct in its naming. To her knowledge, all her kids celebrated Christmas so any veil thrown over the holidays by overly sensitive administrators was thin at best. The children were allowed to exchange a gift of $10 or less with another student whose name they had drawn from a Santa's cap. The gift exchange was as chaotic and exciting as it is every year and the energy the kid's drew from the cookies and Kool-Aid seemed enough to power the city's electric grid for a month! But Mary loved this about children this age and with the exception of a few, as there is always one or two who must be reigned in, she too had a marvelous time. She had received token gifts of appreciation from most of the children and those which weren't consumable, she put in a box, labeled, and put away to look back on when she retired.

Upon entering her house, Mary went straight to the birdcage where a canary resided and whistled to the bird to say hello. The bird fluttered its wings and began singing a beautiful song. Mary and Ted had owned countless canaries since their first, as a canary's lifespan in captivity wasn't very long. However, this latest version was the best entertainer of them all. He seemed to cherish the moment when Mary arrived at the house. Something like a dog barking and wagging its tail, the canary would make small little jumps on its perch and sing as long as Mary stayed near the cage. Its domicile was located in the kitchen, which made clean up easier, as the birds tend to be quite messy and their feathers, seeds, and excrement easily found their way to the tiled floor. Additionally, since this bird only sang in Mary's company, it benefitted her to stay in the kitchen and begin preparing dinner before she changed her clothes.

She didn't usually hear from Ted until after he had eaten dinner and returned to his hotel late in the evening. This allowed Mary to take care of any bills that needed paying or chores that always seemed in desperate need of completion. She would eat her dinner with the company of the television, which she could easily see in the family room from the dining nook located just off the kitchen. After dinner, she would unwind a bit before cleaning the kitchen and settling into her favorite chair to grade assignments and prepare for the next day's lessons.

After preparing her lesson plans, Mary looked at the clock and saw that Ted's phone call was well overdue. Not that this was terribly unusual, as she knew the weather was bad throughout the State and that he was most likely delayed. However, he usually texted her cell phone to let her know he was detained. Naturally, she began to fear that he was in a car accident and turned on the local news to see if there was any news of winter related travel problems. She had to wait through countless commercials and trite news stories before reports on the weather and the havoc it was causing came on. Indeed, the icy weather was creating travel problems in the State and many highways were temporarily shut down until they could be safely treated. No doubt that this is what happened to Ted and he was temporarily stuck on some backwoods road, she thought. She decided to put any bad thoughts from her mind and simply wait for him to call. He always did and tonight should be no different.

Several hours passed and Mary became more worried with each passing minute. She had tried calling him several times, only to have her call transferred to voice mail. Texting him netted no response either. By midnight, she was nearly beside herself in worry and didn't know what to do. She tried to rationalize his lack of communication but her senses screamed that there was something wrong. This simply was not like Ted under any circumstance. She decided to try to go to bed, turning her mind to her nightly routine of getting ready for sleep.

A short time later the doorbell rang and she rushed to answer it. She hesitantly opened it and seeing a sheriff standing on the porch, nearly fainted. Regaining her senses and speaking in what she felt was her strongest, most natural voice said, "Can I help you, Sheriff?"

The male voice that answered was forceful and direct. "Good evening, ma'am, Are you Mrs. Stuart?"

All her strength left her at this salutation and she began to shake.

In a broken voice she replied, "Yes, sir."

"Mrs. Stuart, I'm Sheriff Adkins of the Warren County Sheriff's department and I'm afraid I have some terrible news to report. Your husband, Ted, has been taken to the Ripley Memorial Hospital where he was pronounced dead of massive brain trauma."

Mary's doorway began to spin and she started seeing spots. Her breathing stopped and she knew she was just seconds away from passing out. Uncontrollable gasping was all that she could muster in response to the Sheriff's news. Every effort to pronounce a syllable produced small grunts as she tried in vain to stop the sobbing that was forming deep within her.

Anticipating that she would not take the news well and having been on the end of many calls such as this, the Sheriff knew there was little comfort he could bring her. His training and experience told him to quickly give her facts and then leave so she could react as her nature intended.

"Mrs. Stuart, I know this is shocking news and I must ask that you bear with me for a moment or two. First of all, I'm going to give you my cell phone number so you can reach me anytime. Do you have a pen and paper to write it down?"

As the news sank further into her consciousness, Mary began to mutter, "No, no, no."

Sheriff Adkins responded forcefully, "Mrs. Stuart, are you saying, "no", you don't have a pen and paper?" He wanted her to focus on the task before she completely broke down.

"No, what happened to him?" she replied meekly.

"As we understand it, the Sheriff's department in Union County found him at a job site after his company reported him missing. Evidently, he was struck by a mechanical part on the pump while he was working on it. The sheriff up there thinks he might have slipped on the ice. The conditions are very bad, you know. I have several phone numbers to give you so I suggest we find some paper to write the information down."

Mary shook herself for a second or two and stumbled to the kitchen for a pad of paper and pen she kept on the counter near the phone. Sheriff Adkins followed her into the house.

"Yes," she numbly stammered, "I have it right here."

The sheriff gave her his number and instructions to call under any circumstances if she needed his assistance. He then gave her the Union County Sheriff's number and a contact name in the hospital's morgue to make arrangements to identify Ted's body. For a brief moment, she felt relieved when she heard the body must be identified as this might mean there was uncertainty surrounding the man lying there.

She quickly uttered, "Does this mean that it might not be Ted?"

"I'm sorry, Mrs. Stuart. We're confident that it is your husband. Identification is a formality. Do you understand my instructions?" responded the Sheriff.

She nodded yes, seemingly aware that Sherriff Adkins was standing behind her but the Sheriff knew she wasn't processing the information well.

"Mrs. Stuart, do you understand my instructions?" he asked again.

This time she answered, "Yes", turned and looked at the Sheriff with empty eyes with widened, black pupils. Realizing that she was going into shock, he walked over to the kitchen counter, took a glass by the sink and filled it with water. He brought it to her and asked her to drink the entire contents. This forced Mary to regain some presence in the moment and her pupils dilated back to normal size.

"Mrs. Stuart," he began again. "It isn't a good idea to be alone right now, is there anyone else here?"

She shook her head no.

"Then I will stay here with you as long as you like. It's late in the evening and it might not be easy to find a friend or family to come at this hour."

Mary looked at the Sheriff as her eyes started to well and shook her head no again.

"Thank you, Sheriff, but I want to be alone right now. You may leave." she answered with a muddled and confused look on her face as she walked him to the front door.

It went against his instincts to leave but the Sheriff had no choice when shown the door. He decided to go back to his car and spend the rest of the night in front of her residence in case she needed help. He would check back in on her in the morning.

After closing the front door, Mary fell to the floor and released the anguish that only the desperately wounded heart knows. Her deep, guttural sobs and shuddering breathing convulsed in waves of remorse. She lost ability to control her extremities and she lay in a lump upon the tile entry. She cried for hours, never moving from the spot. Visions of her husband alive, young, and vibrant clashed with imagined scenes of him lying on a slab in a mortuary, alone and cold. These contradictive thoughts only wrought more pain and agony.

As morning light broke upon the house, Mary knew she must pull herself up from the floor and move. She pushed her hands against the cold, hard surface and began to wobbly rise to her knees. A wave of nausea overcame her and she vomited. She remained on her hands and knees for a short time and slowly rose to her feet, knowing that her life, from this moment forward, had far less meaning.

Chapter 10

"There's an easygoing nature that comes with a perspective of things that aren't as important as we make them sometimes." —Marguerite Moreau

Mary felt a soft nudging from an unknown hand as she jolted from her unconscious state. She felt a wave of panic overtake her as her dream's emotions stayed with her even though the vision of that fateful day had left. Her heart ached for Ted as though he had just left her; evoking the concept that the fabric of time and memories share no common thread. As she came to her senses, she quickly recalled that she hadn't wanted to sleep this last day and the pain of personal loss was heightened by the pain of lost moments. She now regretted the shot of morphine that Matitha had given her. "Why can't there be a moment of balance in this world," she thought, "where feeling good didn't come at some expense?"

"I'm so tired..." Mary mumbled to no one in particular.

Hearing this, the aide that had come to retrieve her misunderstood Mary's intent and apologized for waking her.

"I'm sorry I had to wake you, Mrs. Stuart. But it's lunchtime and I'm s'posed to take you to the dining room." said a young man's voice.

She couldn't see the aide as he had quickly settled behind the wheelchair after seeing her awake. He tilted the chair to a more natural seating position and turned it in the direction of the hall she had traveled earlier in the day. He quickly moved the wheelchair down the corridor. He was undoubtedly in a hurry as the rooms seemed to whiz by her peripheral vision. She had noticed that the male aides tended to push the wheelchairs too fast. It appeared their rampant testosterone levels left young men unwilling to meander or move at casual speeds. Everything was a race, even if it didn't matter if she arrived at the dining hall now or five minutes from now. The schoolteacher in her couldn't let a teaching moment pass and she firmly requested that he slow down before they hurt someone coming out of a room. He apologized and reduced their speed.

A more sedated pace afforded Mary the opportunity to quickly gaze into rooms as they passed them. Seeing the various stages of life's end left her pitying the poor souls who resided in them. From one room came a gentle, monotonous moaning that must grow tiresome to anyone that remained within earshot. Past another room, she heard and saw a machine running that provided oxygen for its user. As quickly as this rooms passes, she is upon another that reeks so badly that she must momentarily hold her breath. "How awful." she thought, "Isn't that person aware of the stench?"

Her mind wandered for a moment as she recalled a moment in her past when the septic system that removed sewage from her childhood home backed up into their basement. She remembered how terrible the smell was but how she had gotten used to it quickly, not noticing it until she had left the house and re-entered. Perhaps that is how it is with this person.

On and on, they passed room after room of suffering, faceless people. Some residents along the way were in the hall or community areas smiling and engaging in jovial conversations with each other; giving notice to the fact that there was still much life here to be enjoyed. She wondered about their lives and how their circumstances might differ from hers. She also wondered if they wanted out as badly as she did.

Although the morphine had killed the sharper edge of pain, she still felt the deeper, continuous ache she had grown accustomed to. One nice thing about this or any nursing home was the lack of threshold transitions from room to room. This meant less jarring of her wheelchair and consequentially, less bumping and the knifing pain it caused for her. When they arrived at the dining room, Mary saw Tabitha bending over a resident's chair talking to her. Tabitha caught Mary's eye, smiled and winked at her. She held up her finger in an effort to say she would be over to help Mary in a minute.

The aide deposited Mary and her wheelchair at the same table she had eaten from that morning. Mary was happy that she always sat in the same spot at the same table. It was one of the few certainties in her day. She also benefited from having her back relatively close to a wall. She liked to look out at the room of people and watch them as they ate. More importantly though, she despised it when an aide would come, unannounced, from behind and start to talk to her or move her chair. She didn't like being startled and sitting near a wall allowed her to see who was approaching her.

She didn't have to wait long for Tabitha to come to her, beaming as though she was approaching a pile of gold. Most of the aides were very good about smiling, genuine or not, while others were simply naturally friendly. Tabitha fell into the latter category. She had the gleam in her eye that betrayed earnestness. Mary naturally responded in kind while wondering if the sparkle in her eye still existed.

"HI, MARY!" Tabitha shouted from a few tables over as she approached. "Long time, no see!" she said through a giggle.

Tabitha's natural glow helped relax Mary a bit and she actually felt hungry for the first time that day.

"Hi Tabitha, it's good to see you again. You're a sweet girl." replied Mary.

Tabitha had arrived next to Mary's wheelchair and crouched down to get a better face-to-face angle to talk. For whatever reason, whether it be the lateness in the day or the result of such an impressive first meeting at breakfast, Tabitha felt a much stronger connection with Mary than she did earlier in the day. It surprised her at how quickly she had come to like Mary.

"More chocolate pie?" asked Tabitha as she settled next to Mary.

Mary chuckled, "Eventually, but they gave me a shot a while ago that either got rid of some of my pain or made me hungry. Whichever it is, I want some real food."

"Oh Lord, Mary." continued Tabitha in her sweet chortled voice. "You're at the wrong restaurant! I'll grab my car and we'll get you outta here!"

Both girls, the young with a whole life ahead of her and the aged with only hours left, laughed at Tabitha's droll suggestion. While it was too early for "gallows" humor, perhaps Mary and Tabitha sensed that stepping away from the inevitable would be a bad play during Mary's lunch.

"That's my girl!" laughed Mary in stuttered gasps. "I knew I could count on you. Perhaps you could get me to a Taco Bell for my last meal. Jesus broke bread at his last supper; I'll break wind at mine!"

Tabitha nearly tottered over her heels laughing at the mental image of Mary eating burritos and farting her contempt at a world that had broken her. They both laughed loud and long enough to draw looks of curiosity from other dining residents who were cognizant enough to recognize a good time being had and stares of ire from other aides absent mindedly going through their dining room routine.

As their laughter subsided, Tabitha took Mary's hand and asked if she had always been so funny. Mary's eyes slightly glazed over as she looked into a past that only she now knew. Had she been funny throughout her life? She recalled her daddy's wit and the word play that she and her mother endured in his amusement. Undoubtedly, some of that must have rubbed off on her. But she never really considered herself funny.

"I don't suppose I've ever been funny. At least, not that I'm aware of." she sighed. "But I am hungry and since I don't suppose you were serious about high tailing it outta here, I guess I'd better let you get me some food. Please tell me they have some of those thin, round slices of turkey smothered in tasteless gravy!" Mary said in her most sarcastic voice.

Tabitha grinned and stared at Mary. She suddenly wished that she could get to know Mary better. But knowing that Mary would soon be gone, she stifled her desire and bowed her head in mock submission, replying,

"Your wish is my command. One order of tasteless turkey and gravy coming your way."

Rising to her feet and still smiling and chuckling inwardly at their conversation, Tabitha left the table with the promise of a quick return. Mary watched her lithely move across the room, avoiding chairs, wheelchairs, tables, and servers with the smooth agility of a cat. She disappeared through the swinging kitchen door, leaving Mary watching it flap to and fro until it nearly came to a stop. Before it could completely come to a rest, another aide had given it an unseen shove from the opposite side and the door flew open only to repeat the closing cycle again. She watched this dance many times hoping to see the door come to a complete rest but it never did. In the past, something like this might have slightly agitated her, as she liked issues resolved. However, today was different and the door could continue its exercise while Mary watched in awe.

Giving up hope of a sudden stoppage of kitchen traffic and the peace it would bring to the ever-swinging door, Mary averted her eyes out the windows at the far end of the room. There wasn't much to see out the windows as they faced the parking lot of the nursing home. Grills and headlights from the front end of cars seemed to gaze into the dining room, expressionless and unimpressed with its activities. The day outside appeared to be pretty as the sun was brightly shining and the green shrubs barely visible across the parking lot gently swayed in a light breeze. Other than those few things, there wasn't much for Mary to see outside.

Mary had long ago considered her admittance to the nursing home something of a jail sentence. Much like a prisoner, because of her inability to ambulate or propel her wheelchair, she was confined to whatever space the staff of the nursing home dictated. Her bedroom was her cell, replete with toilet and metal bars around her bed. She could watch TV in her "cell" but little else. When the time was right, Matitha or another aide would come and move her to her meal. They fed her and then placed her somewhere within the confines of the nursing home where she waited for the next stop of the daily routine. This she did, day after day, for the past four and a half years. In a sense, she wasn't much different than the ever-swinging kitchen door. She wondered if it was tired, too.

Guests would come and go, but not for Mary. Her parents and husband long gone and with no children to care, Mary was left utterly alone in imprisonment. She would sometimes eaves drop on conversations between other residents and their visitors, hoping to feel some sense of family or community love but she would be whisked away by staff taking her to her next station in the facility. She never bothered getting to know other residents in the facility. They tend to come and go in this place so why bother? She had experienced enough loss in her life now and adding temporary friends with unavoidable destinies, seemed useless and emotionally depleting.

Tabitha returned from the kitchen carrying a plate and pulled a chair up next to Mary's right side. It had been determined earlier in the day that Mary was right-handed and preferred to have her meals fed to her from that side. In a weak effort of therapy, Mary was instructed to place both hands on Tabitha's as she raised the fork or spoon to her mouth. The effect was twofold. It helped Mary's arms from stiffening from lack of use throughout the day and it gave her an illusion of confidence as she was making efforts to feed to herself.

"I hope you like this..." Tabitha said. "I wish I could tell you that the cook chose the best pieces for you but since there are no best pieces, it would be a lie."

Mary smiled and chewed the food. It met her satisfaction, albeit her pleasure level was a low bar to clear when it came to nursing home food.

"Tabitha," she said between morsels, "tell me about yourself."

Tabitha hesitated for a moment, her hand and Mary's hands frozen in space as she pondered the request. After a second, she replied,

"I'm not sure there is much to tell. What ya see is what ya get with me. I work here and like it for now. But I don't know what I want to do or anything like that. I just kinda live in the moment, you know?"

Mary nodded her head approvingly and continued the conversation.

"How old are you?"

"I'm twenty three."

Mary raised her eyebrows in surprise as she had thought Tabitha was much younger than that.

"Oh, you're older than you look. I figured you to be a teenager." Mary continued.

"Yep, I get that a lot. I figure they won't stop carding me at the bars until I'm fifty at this rate!" she giggled.

Mary chuckled with her. The natural response would be to follow with the standard line that aging slowly is a good thing but Mary was confident that Tabitha had heard that bit of wisdom many times.

"I don't see a ring," said Mary, "is there a man in your life?"

Tabitha looked into Mary's eyes and both felt a strong emotional tug as Tabitha's eyes appeared to sadden a bit. Tabitha put the utensil on the table indicating a need for a break from the feeding. She then laid her hands in her lap.

"Not any more." she said still looking into Mary's eyes. "I had a boyfriend for a couple of years and we broke up a few months ago. His name was Mack."

"Mack is an interesting name..." Mary answered.

"Yeah, it was short for McKenzie. McKenzie was his last name and everyone called him Mack. Even his parents, which I always thought was kinda weird. I mean, who calls their son by his last name, right?"

Mary nodded.

"Anyway," continued Tabitha, "he broke up with me one day. Just left a voicemail on my cell phone that he was leaving and I wouldn't see him anymore. No reason, no excuse. Just goodbye and have a nice life."

Tabitha looked away from Mary and then scanned the room. She was visibly shaken and obviously needed a moment to compose herself. Mary watched her with pity, knowing what it felt like to lose a loved one. She wondered how close the couple had actually been. She gave Tabitha a few moments before inquiring further.

"We all know the feeling of heartbreak that comes from romantic breakups." Mary consoled. "I'm sure you will find a far better replacement and have a wonderful life with him."

Tabitha turned back towards Mary. Her eyes had nearly filled with tears and she wiped them with her hands. After a brief sniffle, she plaintively looked into Mary's eyes.

"How can you know that," she said. "Mack was everything I wanted in a guy. He was fun, handsome, and seemed to genuinely care for me. I mean, he did the nicest things for me that nobody has ever done. I just don't want to go on without him."

Mary was alarmed at the sorrow Tabitha felt at the loss of her boyfriend. She couldn't relate as her only boyfriend was Ted and they had lived a wonderful life together. She always thought her friends were silly the way they fawned over the next boyfriend to enter their lives. So much so, that she never took any of her friend's relationships seriously until it led to marriage. Tabitha's sudden change from perky to sullen had stunned Mary. She actually worried that Tabitha might harm herself. Perhaps her weight problem stemmed from some sort of depression. As Mary considered these possibilities she felt compelled to help Tabitha.

"Tabitha, you mustn't fixate on the loss. You have so much life to live and I can promise you that things will get better. I know how it feels to lose someone. When my husband, Ted, died, I felt there was nothing left for me. Depressing days were followed by depressing weeks and months. But in time, I found joy in living again and you will too."

Tabitha put forth great effort to smile at Mary's advice; however, she was still suffering great emotional pain and felt compelled to contradict Mary.

"That doesn't seem right coming from you. Aren't you ending your life because you have nothing left to live for?" Tabitha asked pointedly.

Mary paused for a moment and looked down into her lap. This day was proving to be far more difficult than she imagined. The coincidence and irony of what had just occurred was not lost on her. Tabitha was right, of course. Why should Tabitha take counsel from someone who had declared her own life unworthy? For that matter, shouldn't she consider heeding her own advice?

Absolutely not, she thought. The two situations were not remotely similar. Tabitha is experiencing what nearly everyone must deal with in youth. Growth is always hard and at times, things like this feel earth shattering. Nevertheless, we grow, becoming stronger and wiser from it. But what Mary was experiencing was entirely different. She had already lived a full life and her days were quickly coming to an end whether she interceded on her own behalf or not. She was not giving up on life for she had none to give up on. Tabitha, however, at a tender age of twenty-three with great health and vigor, has a wonderful life ahead of her.

Mary looked up from her lap and directly into Tabitha's eyes and spoke with the authority that decades of teaching had taught her. She wanted so badly to raise a finger at Tabitha but settled on sharing her most disdainful look.

"You know nothing of pain, young lady. When you live sixty more years, you and I can chat about that." Mary paused to let her words sink in. "My life is over. If all you kind people were to stop caring for me and pushed me out the front door and said, "Go live." I wouldn't make it through tomorrow, would I? That is obvious enough, is it not? What I'm doing is accelerating the process by a few months. Nothing more."

Tabitha looked down in embarrassment for she knew she had unfairly crossed a line with Mary. What was worse for her was that she really liked Mary and didn't want her to be angry with her. She felt tremendously small in Mary's midst now.

Mary continued, drawing upon many such conversations she had had through the years with students of all ages. "I understand your loss but I challenge you to accept it and grow past it. In the brief moments I've shared with you today, I can see you are a difference maker in this world. This planet needs more Tabitha's so please don't let me or yourself down by giving into self-pity."

Tabitha looked up from her lap, reached across Mary, and hugged her. She sniffled and wiped away what remained of her tears and then hugged Mary one more time.

"Thank you, Mary. I feel certain that I'm losing someone more important than Mack today."

She paused, quickly turned her head and in her best effort to put forth a positive attitude replied,

"BUT, you need your dessert and I had the cook hold back two more pieces of chocolate pie for you so I'd better go get 'em. " Tabitha sprang to her feet and hurried through the dining room again, although her stride was not as confident nor her footing as sure.

Mary watched her go and smiled. She knew Tabitha would be alright. Tabitha is much stronger than she knows, thought Mary. But the exchange with Tabitha had worn off the lasting effects of morphine and she was beginning to feel back spasms again. It wouldn't be long before the pain would shoot through her hips and shoulders. With very little time left in her day, Mary would forego any more pain medication.

Chapter 11

"I still find each day too short for all the thoughts I want to think, all the walks I want to take, all the books I want to read, and all the friends I want to see." —John Burroughs

Tabitha kept to her promise and returned with two pieces of chocolate pie. Mary barely had the appetite to eat one so she knew that she couldn't finish two. However, given that this was her last meal, she was resolved to eat every crumb of one of the slabs in front of her.

"Tabitha, it was so sweet of you to bring me two but I don't think I can eat them both. Would you grab a fork and eat the other with me?"

Tabitha looked around the room for a supervisor as she was prohibited from eating any resident's food. Not seeing anyone of authority, she grabbed a fork from one of the empty place settings at the table and swung around wide-eyed at Mary with a sly smile on her face.

"I think that's a great idea!" she enthusiastically said. "But don't tell nobody!'

Mary smiled as she fondly recalled her high school teacher and replied,

"You mean '*anybody*'. Don't worry, '*nobody*' will know."

Mary nearly choked herself in laughter on the first bite after correcting Tabitha's grammar. She hadn't done this in years. The reason for doing it now was a bit of a humorous mystery to her and fun to boot. She swallowed the bite and while Tabitha took a bite of her own, she continued,

"Sorry about that. Old habits die slowly, they say. I was once a schoolteacher and I spent a great deal of my day correcting grammar. I meant nothing of it."

"I see," smiled Tabitha. "You can correct me. I don't mind."

The two continued to eat their pie and talk about unimportant things. After ten minutes or so, the dessert was finished and Matitha appeared in the dining room, stomping in her particular way to where Mary was finishing her last bite.

"Mama, I sees you about done. Are you ready to go?" barked Matitha.

Mary looked at Matitha and could see she had struck an authoritative attitude since their last meeting. It was wondrous for Mary to behold how many moods nurses and aides went through in their day at work. They weren't aware of it as she, for she got to see them in small snippets separated by time and events unknown. All she could see was that there was a change from the last parting and she wondered what had occurred in the meantime.

"Yes, Matitha. I'm done."

Mary asked Tabitha to hold her hand one last time and the two looked at each other as if to seal the memory of each other's face forever. Mary could sense the uneasiness of the moment, wryly smiled and said,

"Don't smoke cigarettes and for God's sake, don't get anymore tattoos. You are too beautiful to ruin your body that way."

Not expecting this sage advice, Tabitha burst out a loud laugh that caught everyone in the room by surprise.

"I won't," she promised with her eyes sparkling as they had earlier. "I'll miss you, Mary. Goodbye." With those words spoken, she rose to her feet and jaunted off to the kitchen again.

Matitha looked on with amusement at the parting and her abrupt personality of the moment melted away in to astonishment.

"What on earth was that about?" she asked

Mary smiled up at Matitha and simply replied, "I think I made a new friend today."

Matitha bent over to see if the brakes on Mary's wheelchair were engaged, saw that they were and moved to the back of the chair to release them. While gently pulling Mary back from the table, careful not to bump her body or the chair for fear of the pain it would cause Mary, she began to push her towards the exit.

"Mama, I do declare. You could make friends anywhere's you wanted to. People just naturally likes you."

Mary looked straight ahead with a small smile on her lips.

"What's next on our agenda?"

As though Mary hadn't said anything, Matitha continued her thoughts.

"I's knew it from the first time I saw you. You know how you get that feelin' about some people? The one that just shouts, 'this is a good person'. Well, that's how I felt about you. You radiate goodness, Mama and folks around here are gonna miss ya."

Matitha continued on as she pushed the wheelchair into the hallway that Mary had already travelled several times today.

"I know you know it's time to go talk with the preacher man in the chapel. He's such a young man so I'm not sure how much he knows about the scriptures. I hope he can give you some comfort."

"Oh!" she blurted loudly. "I's forgot to tells you that the Psychiatrist that okay'd your request will be there, too. He has to make sure you's still in a right mind. Of course, if they asked me, I's say you wasn't or you's wouldn't be makin' this choice. But nobody asks Matitha nothin' even though she knows everybody's mind in this place."

Mary couldn't help smiling at Matitha's rant as she has heard similar ones many times before. It was part of Matitha's charm to say the least. However, her smile quickly faded as a new wave of pain was suddenly upon her. This pain came from her hips as she had slightly twisted when Matitha had to jerk the chair to the side to avoid a resident in a power wheelchair coming out of his room.

Matitha knew immediately that the maneuver had hurt Mary as she saw Mary's body tense up. Angry at the resident who had caused the near accident, she shouted at him.

"Mr. Akers! That'll be the last time you nearly runs someone over in that chair! I'm goin' straight to Nurse Cathy and tell her what you did!"

Nurse Cathy was the Director of Nursing in the facility and was responsible for the welfare and safety of all the residents. She didn't like having motorized wheelchairs in the facility to begin with because of the safety issues it raised for every resident. However, the facility had maintained a freedom of movement policy that forbade any restrictions on resident's who could safely propel manual or power wheelchairs. Mr. Akers wasn't nearly the threat to himself or anyone else that Matitha made him out to be in this unfortunate meeting. It would have been difficult for him to exit his room any more slowly than he had. The nursing home was a busy place with many people in the halls at times. Absent traffic signals to regulate the entry and exit of residents from their rooms, near misses were just the nature of the beast.

Matitha continued to push Mary's wheelchair down a few more hallways before turning to go into the chapel. Unfortunately for Mary, the chapel was carpeted and required the transition bump from the smooth vinyl flooring of the hall into the inner sanctum. Matitha did her best to take the bump slowly but the overall weight and size of the chair necessitated an abrupt push to roll over the threshold. The sudden jerk of the chair sent waves of pain through Mary's body and she began to see stars as she nearly fainted from the pain. As she regained her senses she again questioned herself about the wisdom of foregoing pain medication.

"I'm so sorry, Mama." said Matitha. "I did my best on that bump."

Mary gritted her teeth and tried to allay Matitha's regret.

"It's okay, Matitha. It's my fault for not taking the pain meds."

The sanctuary was a vast departure from any room in the nursing home. Although small by church standards, it was quite large for a nursing home of this size. It was hexagonal in shape with two sections of pews about eight feet long separated by a center aisle. The side walls were painted white and accented with thin wood beams that rose from the floor to a ten foot ceiling in a asymmetrical checkerboard pattern. The front of the room had a slightly elevated stage with a lectern situated in the center. Directly behind the lectern, the exterior wall of the room had two floor-to-ceiling stained glass windows, featuring two doves on either side clasping a length of cloth in their beaks separated by a wall with a large cross on it.

Two men in the chapel looked up from a conversation they were having in the first pew. The younger man, dressed in the robes of a minister, quickly rose to his feet and hurried down the seven rows of pews to assist Matitha. He arrived in time to hear Mary's comment about her medications but could do more than look on in pity.

"Hello, Mary." he serenely said. "It's always a pleasure to see you."

Mary raised her eyes as she fought the spasms racking every nerve of her body and in her strongest voice that could easily be mistaken for a whisper replied,

"You too, Pastor Stephens."

Pastor Stephens was a young minister of the Lutheran faith. Having finished seminary school just a few years earlier, Pastor Stephens had chosen to serve nursing homes in the Vicksburg area. Although Northern Oaks was a secular nursing home, its owners were of the Lutheran faith and had affiliations with the local diocese. Pastor Stephens served as the residential minister for the nursing home. He was sensitive to the fact that he was ministering to people of all faiths and tried valiantly to keep his message to fundamental Christian mores embraced by all Christian faiths. Of course, many residents and families brought in their personal ministers to visit and Pastor Stephens welcomed and accommodated them as best he could. First and foremost though, he considered this sanctuary and the residents of Northern Oaks his to take care of.

"Mary, why don't we go up to the front pew where I can sit while we talk? Matitha, do you mind?"

"No sir, Pastor Stephens. I'll just push her on up there and leave. I do say, though, I loves this chapel and wish I could stay all day in here!" Matitha said as she pushed the wheelchair down the center aisle.

"I'm happy to hear that Matitha." replied the minister. "You know you're always welcome to come in and worship on your breaks, providing it's available of course."

"I know that but I never thinks about it during the course of my day. Just too busy..."

Her voice trailed off as she situated Mary's wheelchair parallel to the pew so that she could look to her right to see the cross and stained glass windows. She locked the brakes on the wheelchair and hurried out of the chapel.

Meanwhile, the other man across the aisle had sat quietly throughout the activity, observing the relationships of the three. Dr. Abrahms had practiced psychiatry for nearly twenty years before giving it up to work for the State of Mississippi. His decision to leave private practice was predicated on maintaining his own sanity. Although physicians are trained to emotionally disconnect from their patients, some psychiatrists have a very difficult time doing so. They try to maintain regular office hours like most doctors, but the needs of their patients couldn't be conveniently parceled into 8 hour days. His evenings and weekends were constantly interrupted with emergencies that demanded his attention thus leaving his life in a constant torrent of difficulty and stress.

After resigning his practice, he managed to secure the position of Department Head of Emotional Services for the State of Mississippi through contacts he knew in the Capitol. It was mostly a administrative position that required very little medical training and a great deal of organizational skill. Not satisfied with the direction of his career and the lack of medical stimulation, he chose to accept one of the five positions the State created with the Death with Dignity Law, interviewing candidates for physician-assisted suicide. Although the position was created to ascertain the sanity of those requesting euthanasia, it allowed Dr. Abrahms the opportunity to explore the human mind during the final moments of fatal exhaustion. He hoped to write a treatise on the matter when he had accumulated enough research. Fortunately, he had no qualms about releasing the petitioners to their desired deaths as he had witnessed enough suffering of the mind through his practice to completely understand the need for eternal rest.

From this point on, Pastor Stephens took the lead.

"Mary, I believe you've met Dr. Abrahms, right?"

Mary nodded her head and looked up at the doctor approaching her chair. For whatever reason, she pitied this man and his job. How horrible it must be for him to have to facilitate releasing people to their demise, even if it is their wish. She couldn't understand how he possibly maintained a happy life doing so.

"Doctor, I hope you're having a nice day." she said to him even now, despite all of her pain, trying to help him feel better about his task.

"Thank you, Mary. I am." he said succinctly. "I hope you understand the necessity of my being here. The State of Mississippi requires that you be of sane mind before the procedure can take place. You qualified in that regard after our last meeting, therefore, this interview will be very short. Do you understand?"

Mary did not like the coldness with which he presented the premise of the discussion but nodded her head affirmatively, weakly replying yes. Dr. Abrahms proceeded to ask her basic questions about her name, age, and family history. Ascertaining that her memory was intact, he continued on with questions about her current living arrangements and how she felt about her care givers. Mary responded as best she could as her pain and discomfort were increasing due to her being in her current sitting position too long. She stated that she liked the nursing home and her care givers and would recommend the place to anyone who asked.

Meanwhile, Pastor Stephens sat by, holding Mary's hand throughout the interrogation. He looked from Mary to the doctor and back again multiple times, utterly heart broken over what he was witnessing. He feared the moment the doctor would leave for he wasn't sure what he could say to aid Mary. The situation was horrible for him to bear.

Dr. Abrahms concluded his questioning and spent a few moments writing notes on a form. Mary turned her head towards Pastor Stephens and asked him to reposition the tilt in her wheelchair. Happy to be of service, he sprang to his feet and did as Mary asked. Her most intense pain immediately subsided and she smiled at him as he returned to his seat. The doctor looked up from his notes and began.

"I'm all finished here so I will leave you two to talk. Mary, as you know, the event will occur in the privacy room located in a quiet section of the nursing home. I will be there ensuring the proper medications are delivered without any problems. You will be the one that presses the button releasing the drugs. I can assure you that you will feel no pain. You will simply nod off to sleep as you would if you were receiving surgery anesthesia. You may at any time call this off and all of us here would be happy that you did. However, the decision is yours. Do you wish to proceed?"

Pastor Stephens squeezed her hand hoping she would feel his affection for her and call off the affair. Mary grimaced at the pressure and turned her head towards Pastor Stephens. They shared a few moments of locked eyes and then Mary returned her face towards the doctor.

"Yes, doctor, I wish to proceed."

Having heard what he needed to hear, Dr. Abrahms packed up his briefcase and left.

Overcome with passion, Pastor Stephens waited for the doctor to leave before imploring Mary to reconsider.

"I know I can't feel what you do but you are so vital and full of life. I've asked many people in this home about you. They all tell me how wonderful and pleasant you are. You are still a blessing to many on this earth." he said in his most earnest voice.

Mary's eyes began to swell with tears. What she had felt with great conviction was melting in this moment. She did love life and she cared deeply for the few people she could share it with now. Her pain was great, unbearable at times, but the medications did quell it for brief moments throughout the day. Wasn't she stronger than this?

"Pastor Stephens," she implored with eyes glistening, "please pray for me."

The minister bowed his head at her request and searched deeply into his soul to find the right words for Mary. He was well past judging her or praying for her forgiveness as he knew in his heart that Mary deserved a special place in heaven. He only wished to comfort her and himself through this ordeal.

"Dear Heavenly Father," he began,

"We come to you in this hour of need to request peace for Mary. Your love has shown us that we mustn't take the blessing of life lightly but embrace it with the strength of our fathers who have done so before us. Judge not Mary on her decision, but reward her for a life spent helping others and for truly professing her love and dedication to You. We know, as you promised, that you have prepared a place for all those who love Christ and keep him holy. Mary is ready to share that place with you. Her pain will be gone and all those she has lost before her will be there to welcome her to the realm of everlasting love. We pray that you will give those of us she leaves behind the strength to carry on in her absence and ability to care for others as she has done for so many years. In Jesus' most heavenly name we pray. Amen."

And Mary wept.

She wept for all that she has known and all that will be gone forever. She wept for the lost love of her departed mother and father.

She wept for Ted, who, in the decades that have passed since they met, has not aged since high school. She wept for all the wonderful people who filled her life and the small deeds of kindness they shared. She wept for the birds in the sky and the sun and clouds that silhouetted their flight. She wept for the sensual privations that will soon be denied. In short, she wept for life.

Chapter 12

"Mistakes are the portal of discovery." —James Joyce

"What have I done?" thought Tabitha.

Leaning against the door of a large walk-in refrigerator, Tabitha had the palm of her left hand pressed against her lips and was blankly staring into the kitchen. The last lunch shift was over and activity in the kitchen had settled down to just a few aides moving through the swinging door while the kitchen staff hustled to clean the serving pans and implements that were scattered across the room.

"I can't believe I treated her that way." Tabitha spoke out loud this time to no one in particular. "She's so nice and she's gonna die soon and I crapped all over her... What was I thinking?" Tabitha looked down at the tattoo on her on arm and began to wonder if she was the dragon so boldly imprinted there.

Realizing that she was beginning to make a scene by standing idly in the kitchen area, Tabitha went to the time clock mounted on the wall by the back entrance door and timed out for her afternoon break. Unwilling to hang out in the staff break room where she would be forced to interact with other employees she wasn't ready to get to know, she headed out of the kitchen and into the labyrinth of hallways to make her way to the rear of the building where the exit to the employee parking lot could be found. In fear of breaking rules her very first day, she had moved her car to the employee lot during her morning break.

Once free of the facility, she quickly made her way to her car, unlocked it and positioned herself in the driver's seat. Placing her hands in the proper ten and two position on the steering wheel, she sat and stared out the front windshield.

Her lunch encounter with Mary did not go as she had hoped. She had volunteered to care for Mary today because she felt she could easily look past her imminent death. Almost every Dining Room staff member acted as though Mary had the plague and didn't want to interact with her today. Tabitha attributed this to the fact that they knew her and didn't want to deal with the emotion of knowing that they were about to lose her. But as she thought about it throughout the morning, that rationale didn't quite make sense. They lose residents in the facility all the time, so why would Mary's departure be any different? Surely, they developed a sort of callousness to death in this place.

After her lunch encounter with Mary, Tabitha began to understand. Mary's impending death was like an elephant in the room that everyone knew was there but didn't want to acknowledge. What does one say to someone who is approaching certain death? Do you interact with her about it and try to comfort her, even if you don't know her or her circumstances? Or, do you act like it's a normal day and ignore the obvious and just try to do your best to serve her? Tabitha had settled on the latter and now regretted it. By treating the day as a normal day in a life, she unloaded her own emotional baggage on Mary!

"The poor lady is dying today and I'm ranting about a stupid boyfriend?" Tabitha shouted at the steering wheel of her car, slamming her hand into the horn and causing it to release a short blast. Embarrassed by the noise, she quickly scanned the immediate area to make sure nobody was coming her way to assist her. That would have been icing on the cake after her emotional meltdown with Mary. She began to think she might be losing her mind.

Tabitha sat and replayed the events that had transpired with Mary today. Breakfast had gone amazingly well. She and Mary both seemed to take to each other. The situation regarding the pie was a little rocky at first but Tabitha thought she had handled it with aplomb, displaying a grace and poise beyond what one would have expected of a first day employee.

In fact, Tabitha really like Mary's derring-do as it reminded her a bit of herself. While not necessarily a rule breaker, Tabitha didn't mind stretching the parameters of certain rules if logic dictated it. When she left college, everyone told her that she most likely wouldn't finish. The general rule was that the longer one stayed out and enjoyed life, one lost the rigor and dedication that college required. Tabitha, though, didn't think this would apply to her. However, in retrospect and in a moment of self-awakening, Tabitha realized that she had gone several years without re-enrolling and she was not ready to go back yet. Perhaps she was just another victim of a hubris that didn't think the rules applied to her.

This realization slammed down upon her with amazing force. She was momentarily stunned by the revelation that she probably wouldn't finish school. Her life the past three years had not been about bettering herself, or growing as a person. Instead, it had been about living in the moment, taking advantage of what was given to her as opposed to what she had earned. She had allowed her self-value to come from the strength of Mack's success, which taken from her, left her very little to rely on. Perhaps what was most painful about the loss of Mack was the loss of an identity. She was no longer part of "they" and had lost what it meant to be "me".

The sudden epiphany nearly stopped Tabitha's heart. She gasped at what she had once been; an intelligent, caring, driven person, and what she had now become. Mary was right without even knowing Tabitha. Tabitha was wallowing in self-pity. She had placed all her hope and future in the hands of another and in doing so became a victim when he left her. However, Mack didn't victimize her. Tabitha suddenly realized that she was a victim of her own making.

Yes. She loved Mack. Did that mean that he should have been the center of her existence? Absolutely not, she decided. She was more than just Mack's girlfriend. She was Tabitha! The girl that didn't back down from challenges. The slightly rebellious one that felt rules applied to other people who couldn't exercise self-control. Tabitha knew in this moment, that her life had changed. She felt the tingling of excitement and the flushed cheeks that come from the warmth of feeling good about one's self. She now knew that she could do anything she desired and the rush of adrenaline made her feel robust and energized.

Wizened and amused by the awakening that had just occurred within her, Tabitha began to laugh. Her imagination jumped to her famous Christmas show, Dr. Seuss', "How the Grinch Stole Christmas" and pictured her own heart growing three sizes just then and she laughed some more. She then visualized herself as Scrooge and the feelings he had after his night of ghostly visitations. He turned his life around and she was now convinced she would too.

"But what to do about Mary?" she thought. It is because of her that Tabitha now found new meaning and hope in life. That sweet old woman who remained so sharp and helpful was about to be gone and Tabitha owed her a deep debt of gratitude. "What can I do for her?" contemplated Tabitha.

She didn't know any of the details surrounding Mary's euthanasia. Her supervisor had told her that it was going to happen and that was it. Tabitha made it a point now to find the Nursing Home Administrator and ask if there was anything she could do to help Mary. She then prayed a quick prayer that she fulfill Mary's wishes and make herself useful. Her break almost over, she left the car and quickly set out for the Administrator's office. With the resolve of a titan, her tiny frame bowled through the halls of the nursing home, undeterred by anything that crossed her path.

Chapter 13

"Reason, or the ratio of all we have already known, is not the same that it shall be when we know more." —William Blake

In a corridor near the rear of the nursing home, a former resident's room was being prepared for the euthanasia procedure. The room had been completely remodeled to look and feel like a room that might be found in any house. The walls were repainted from the off-white of a standard room to a warm brown with dark brown molding around it. Printed curtains drawn over the window darkened the room so that a soft light from a center-mounted fixture was its only luminary. Oil paintings of pastoral scenes adorned each wall and tiny knick-knacks were casually placed as they would be in anybody's room. The standard hospital bed that was used throughout the facility was replaced with a four-poster twin bed. On it were ivory sheets and a beige cotton blanket.

Two nurses were busy making connections to a machine placed unobtrusively in a corner of the room. This machine would administer the fatal concoction of drugs that would douse Mary's life. It was the same formula of barbiturate, paralytic and potassium solution used for lethal injections in condemned prisoners. They checked and retested the machine to make sure it was functioning correctly. Assured that it was, they then connected a tube from the machine to a line running from an IV bag hanging from a pole. They moved from the IV to a heart-monitoring machine, turning it on and off to ensure it was operational and ready to play its part in the drama. Once this work was completed, they stood in the corner completely opposite the contraption as though fearful that it would somehow malfunction and execute them by mistake.

Meanwhile, Dr. Abrahms and the nursing home's Administrator went over the details of what would transpire after Mary's death. All the appropriate paperwork was on hand and ready for his signature once he had confirmed her passing. The Administrator assured him that an ambulance crew was standing by to whisk Mary out the side door, bringing little or no attention to this wing of the facility. Once the particulars of the procedure were squared away, Dr. Abrahms and the Administrator made idle chitchat while they patiently waited for Mary's arrival.

****

Pastor Stephens knew better than to try to console Mary. He watched helplessly as she cried, wanting so badly to do something to ease her pain. Alas, he could only hold her hand and pray inwardly that her suffering would be replaced with the joy of heaven.

As Mary tearfully exhausted her remorse, Matitha entered the chapel to inform them that it was time for them to assemble in the privacy room. She quickly ascertained that Mary had been weeping and rushed forward into the sanctuary to hug her. She briefly hoped that Mary had experienced a change of heart but then realized that Mary's sullen eyes didn't reflect any change. Regardless, she grabbed Mary in such a brusque manner of affection that Mary screamed in pain.

Matitha cursed herself for what she had just done. She so loved this fragile flower that it always took great control to not overly express it physically. But she had failed herself and Mary this time and she knew she could only tolerate so much more emotional pain over the impending loss and the toll it was taking on her. She apologized, again and again, for her mistake as she pushed Mary's wheelchair up the aisle, followed by Pastor Stephens, and into the hallway. The trip to the privacy room was a short one and none of the three spoke. The pall of what was to transpire hung over the small group as it made its way down the corridor.

When they arrived at the room, Matitha stopped the wheelchair to say her farewell. She hesitated a few moments after kneeling down to speak with Mary and then started hyperventilating. Her breaths were heavy and fast as she tried to hold back the waves of sadness overtaking her. Mary had been in her care for several years and letting go like this didn't settle well with her. She wished she could be stronger for Mary but it simply wasn't to be.

"Oh, Mama." she huffed. "You know I have to say goodbye here."

Again, she took multiple fast and deep breaths to ward off the tears before going on.

"You knows how much I love you and will miss you, right?" she asked.

Mary nodded her head and through gritted teeth, tenderly replied, "I've never doubted it, Matitha. You have been an angel of mercy and I love you too. Goodbye, my dear girl."

"Goodbye, Mama." Matitha rose and with head down and tears in her eyes, quickly walked down the hall.

Mary heard footsteps hurrying towards them and turned her head to see who was running down the hall. She was surprised to see Tabitha come quickly up to her wheelchair. She arrived breathlessly saying,

"I made it. Oh good. If you don't mind Mary, I want to be with you until the end. I want to hold your hand all the way through if that's okay?"

Mary looked at her in amazement. She had only met this child a few hours ago and didn't understand why she would choose to volunteer for such a gruesome task. However, Mary hadn't given much thought as to who would be there with her in the end. She assumed nobody would be close by. She had considered asking Matitha but then quickly dismissed the idea as too painful for Matitha to bear. She didn't know the Pastor well enough so there was really no one else to turn to.

"Tabitha, you sweet thing." Mary squeaked out between her breaths and waves of pain. "I could never ask you to do such a thing. It will be too hard on you."

Tabitha unleashed the smile she had first displayed when they met that morning and the gleam in her eye shone with the brightness of the sun. There was no denying that this young woman had a wonderful gift of warmth and grace in her mannerisms. Mary was instantly comforted and truly grateful that she had come to help.

Tabitha responded, "Mary, you need me and I want to be here for you. I don't want to ever forget you." Her eyes glistened as she looked directly into Mary's.

"Alright, then. Let's go in." Mary breathlessly said.

Tabitha took position at the back of the wheelchair and pushed it into the room. There were several people in the room that Mary didn't know. Everybody was busy doing something but to Mary, it didn't look like they were really doing anything. None looked up at her except Dr. Abrahms and the Administrator of the Northern Oaks, who stopped their conversation as Mary entered. The Administrator of the nursing home was a tall woman who Mary only knew as Jan. She rarely saw her in the halls and the few times she did, Jan was at a nurse's station talking with the nurses on duty.

Jan came to wheelchair and said, "Hello, Mary. We've done all we can to make this situation as comfortable for you as possible. Is there anything else I can do for you? "

Mary just nodded her head no. She didn't know this woman and didn't want to waste energy talking to her.

"Well, I do hope you will reconsider." she said brusquely.

With that said, Jan left the room.

"Was that disdain in her voice?" wondered Mary

Two of the aides that were working on the equipment around the bed came over to Mary and said they would transfer her to the bed. They didn't bother using a Hoyer Lift. They were strong and easily lifted Mary out of her chair and placed her gently on the bed. The movement, however quick and fluid as it was, racked Mary with pain and her nausea returned. To make matters worse, the mattress on the bed was a regular mattress used in the nursing home and not the air mattress that she slept on. The rigidity of the mattress made every contact point between it and her bones a spot of knifing pain. She had to forcefully respire, breathing deeply and exhaling in slow rhythm, to maintain control of herself. When she settled down some, one of the aides inserted an IV into her left arm.

After they had her successfully settled into the bed, they left without saying anything, leaving the room empty except for Dr. Abrahms and Tabitha. Dr. Abrahms moved close to the head of the bed and gently laid his hand on Mary's shoulder.

"Mary." he said stoically. "This is a very simple procedure. I am going to place this button," motioning to a red button on a pendant at the end of a long cord, "in your right hand. When you are ready, you simply push the red button and the drugs will be released. You will feel no pain and you will quickly go to sleep. The drug that stops your heart is not released until you are completely unconscious. Again, I stress you will not feel a thing."

"I also want to reiterate one last time that you do not have to go through with this. Since Tabitha has offered to stay close to you, I am going to move to the back of the room. If you choose to abort, I will quickly move to disconnect the IV. Do you understand?"

Mary weakly confirmed her understanding. Of course, she didn't comprehend half of what he had just said. She felt her world spinning uncontrollably after he had placed the pendant in her hand. His words were blurred and difficult to comprehend. All she knew for certain was the red button was the death button and it was now resting in her hand.

She began to shake as she felt a wave of coldness grip her body. The tremors she experienced set off pain spasms in her back and hips. The pain was excruciating and it brought her back to reality. Her eyes widened and they darted to find Tabitha.

Tabitha instantly saw the fear in Mary's eyes and grabbed her left hand with both of hers.

"I'm here, Mary. I'm here" she said a voice choked with emotion.

Mary heard and felt Tabitha and a rare moment of painlessness overcame her. She turned her head to look at her. Dear Tabitha. A girl she had only met a few hours ago now meant the world to her. She *was* the world to Mary. Tabitha was the only anchor she had left holding her in a world of suffering and exhausted resources. Mary and Tabitha looked into each others eyes. The old, translucent, if not opaque eyes that had seen so much in a lifetime gazing tenderly into the young, vibrant eyes of naivety.

Mary turned her gaze from Tabitha and stared up at the ceiling. She looked at the soft light emitting from the light fixture and wondered what was next for her. She did not want to die but she did not want to live either. She was caught in an earthly purgatory with no easy escape. She knew what she was walking away from but didn't know what she was heading into. She suddenly realized how tenuous faith is. What seems so certain and easy to believe from afar quickly fades as it draws closer. Was she doing the right thing? Is there a heaven for her or is she simply plunging into nothingness, a candle snuffed out never to light again? A panic began to overtake her and she quickly turned to Tabitha. She was still there holding and caressing Mary's hand while gazing deeply into her eyes with warmth and love.

And then she heard it. A voice from afar. A voice she remembered but couldn't specifically recall spoke out to her and said, "It's time to come home, Mary."

Mary turned her gaze to the ceiling again and pushed the red button. An icy coldness crept up her arm as she felt the fluids enter her blood stream. Her whole body suddenly felt cold and she began to worry that perhaps the doctor was wrong about the drugs putting her to sleep. And then nothingness. The pain was gone and with it a life, no longer worth living, was too.

####

Acknowledgments

I wish to say thank you to my family for their unfailing support as I worked through this project of love. To my daughters I'd like to remind them that a journey's end brings new trails yet unimagined. Never fear the unknown!

A special thanks is necessary to my counsels who helped shaped this story: Adams Steven and Betsy Beyette. Thank you for receiving my work and helping me correct its flaws.

Also, thank you Katie Sloan for your fine book cover design. You are so talented. Always be bold!

Lastly, I would like to acknowledge my special friends and associates in the Midwest Association for Medical Equipment Services, (MAMES). Keep fighting for the well-being of the aged and disabled.

About the Author

Born and raised in Independence, MO, I am proud graduate of Truman High School. After studying three and half years at the University of Missouri-Columbia, I graduated with a Liberal Arts Degree from the University of Missouri-Kansas City.

I founded and spent the majority of my professional career managing a medical equipment company that specialized in Wheelchair Seating and Positioning for the severely disabled.

Besides owning and running my company, I have testified before Congress on the detrimental impacts that certain health care legislation will have on American Seniors. I have also served as a Board Member and President of the Midwest Association for Medical Equipment Services. I worked closely with Senator Pat Roberts of Kansas regarding questions of healthcare legislation and been recommended by him for appointment to the Program Advisory and Oversight Committee for Quality Standards and Competitive Acquisition of Certain Durable Medical Equipment. In short, I have dedicated my life to being a caring advocate for the aged and disabled.

The Canary's Song is not just a story about death, it's a story about life and how each of us impacts one another in ways so subtle, that we doubt their authenticity. I once read that from our first breath forward, we begin a trek towards death. It's what we do between our first breaths and last that defines living. Perhaps this thought is too sanguine as each of us must face struggles in life that slowly drain our will to keep going. However, we must persevere because we can't possibly know what positive influence we can contribute to a soul in need or a world in turmoil. This book was, at times, very difficult for me to write as I bleed eternal optimism and was quite shaken knowing that the end for Mary would come in a way I hoped it wouldn't. But enlightenment sometimes comes at a cost and understanding viewpoints that differ from mine are as important as being true to my own values.

I hope you enjoyed reading <u>The Canary's Song</u> and feel moved to make a difference in your own and others' lives. For we are only here for a short time.